Menace at Mammoth Cave

A Kit Mystery

by Mary Casanova

★ AmericanGirl®

americangirl.com/service

For Winnie and Vivian,
and all who pursue life
with curiosity and courage

Beforever™

The adventurous characters you'll meet in
the BeForever books will spark your curiosity
about the past, inspire you to find your voice
in the present, and excite you about your future.
You'll make friends with these girls as you share
their fun and their challenges. Like you, they are
bright and brave, imaginative and energetic,
creative and kind. Just as you are, they are
discovering what really matters: Helping others.
Being a true friend. Protecting the earth.
Standing up for what's right. Read their stories,
explore their worlds, join their adventures.
Your friendship with them will BeForever.

TABLE *of* CONTENTS

Rumblings of Trouble

chapter 1

STEEL ON STEEL, brakes squealed as the train slowed to a stop. The trip from Cincinnati had been long, but they'd finally arrived at Mammoth Cave.

Kit gazed out her passenger window. "Aunt Millie! There's Charlie!"

In his familiar brown cap, her brother waited under the awning of a whitewashed building edged with bright red flowers.

"Must be feeding him well," Aunt Millie said. "They've put some meat on his bones."

Kit had to agree. Her eighteen-year-old brother looked different in the months since she'd last seen him—older somehow.

She tugged her suitcase from the overhead bin, and when the conductor opened the door, she was waiting on the top step, eager to hop off.

A wall of hot, humid air greeted her.

"Welcome to Mammoth Cave Hotel, young lady!" a gray-haired porter boomed, grabbing her suitcase.

"We're not staying at the hotel," Kit said, tugging it back again. She and Aunt Millie had scrounged enough pennies together for a round-trip train ride, but they didn't have extra for a hotel.

"My apologies, Miss." With that, the porter turned to the next passenger.

In the throng of tourists, Kit felt herself swept up from behind by two strong arms around her waist, twirling her. "Charlie!" she squealed, as one shoe went flying, then the other. "My shoes!"

By the time Charlie set Kit to the ground again, Aunt Millie held Kit's shoes in hand.

"Am I next?" Aunt Millie joked.

Charlie laughed. "If you'd like, Aunt Millie."

"I'd better keep my feet on the ground," she said with a laugh, "but thank you kindly."

Charlie grinned ear to ear. "I can't believe you're both here."

Kit put her hands on her hips. "Anyone who uses the word *peculiar* in a letter to me should know it will make me extra curious. You have to tell me what you meant!"

Charlie laughed. "There's time enough, Kit." He picked up the two suitcases, then trotted off ahead. "Follow me, ladies."

Hurrying behind Charlie, Kit could practically recite his letter from memory. He'd said he was working at one of four camps at the park, and that each camp put out its own newspaper filled with bits of work news and jokes. Then he'd written, *"But, honestly, there are some peculiar things going on around here lately. It's what doesn't get in the papers that's most interesting."*

Kit wanted to know more, but she held her tongue and followed him through a gravel parking lot to a rusty red Ford truck.

"This truck belongs to Joe, one of the guys at camp," Charlie said. "Rents it out for fifty cents a day."

"I'm happy to cover the cost," Aunt Millie said.

"I'll help," Kit added.

The Depression had hit everyone hard in the past few years, but it seemed to Kit that things were finally starting to get better. Dad had finally found part-time work at the airport. Mother had taken in boarders, whose rent had allowed Kit's family to keep their house. And one of the programs President Franklin Roosevelt had launched—the CCC, or Civilian Conservation Corps—had given men like Charlie a job. Each month, Charlie sent home twenty-five dollars of his dollar-a-day pay.

Now it was August 1934, and Kit and her aunt were coming to stay for ten days with Aunt Millie's childhood friend, Miss Pearl, who lived near the Mammoth Cave area where Charlie was working with the CCC.

Charlie tossed their luggage into the truck bed. "Before we head out, I'm going to show you something you've never seen before."

They trekked after Charlie down a path into a hollow. Beside the path, a creek gurgled and flowed. Tall oak and beech trees cast shadows of dappled green and gray. The air cooled degree by degree as they descended. Excitement tiptoed up Kit's spine. Was he going to show them the "peculiar things" he'd mentioned in his letter?

As they came around a bend in the path, a sign read: "Historic Entrance." A bit farther on, a cluster of tourists gathered.

Kit stepped up to a railing. Below, a dark hole gaped like the mouth of an underground monster. Its throat was deep, and it shot out a continuous blast of cold air. A steep set of steps dropped toward its mouth and then leveled off into a path that extended deeper into darkness.

Goose bumps rose on Kit's arms. She watched

as a group of tourists gathered around a man with a helmet and flashlight. "If anyone has a bad heart or is afraid of close spaces, you might want to skip this tour," he began.

Aunt Millie shook her head. "I don't think people are meant to go belowground. It's unnatural."

Charlie laughed. "Yeah, strange things live down there. Fish without eyes."

"Creepy!" Kit said, and made a mental note to find out more. "Did they find fossils of woolly mammoths here?"

"It's called Mammoth Cave because it's so huge," Charlie said. "It's the largest underground cave in the world."

Kit stared. A carpet of ferns surrounded the mouth of the cave. Water trickled in rivulets toward the entrance, then fell off to its side and disappeared belowground. It was scary, but not enough to keep her from wanting to see inside.

"Come on!" she said, heading toward the cave

opening. "What are we waiting for?"

"Hold on!" Charlie laughed. "You have to have a guide, and there isn't enough time now. I still need to get you to the Thatchers' and then get back to camp with the truck."

"Oh, but we're so close," Kit begged.

"Don't worry, Kit," Charlie said with a smile as he turned away. "You'll see it before you go back home."

Reluctantly, Kit pulled herself away from the beckoning cave. She hiked up the hollow and into the baking light of day.

As Charlie eased the truck down a steep road toward a wide ribbon of water, Kit hoped the brakes would hold. "This is the Green River," Charlie said, parking at the water's edge. "Camp's on the other side."

Kit looked around, puzzled. The road simply stopped at the riverbank, and there was no bridge.

"How do we get across?" she asked.

Charlie pointed to a flat-bottomed boat that was just pulling away from the opposite shore. "That's how," he explained. "It's a ferry. You ride across right in your car!"

The boat glided up to shore, and a man in coveralls lowered a ramp. Charlie drove the pickup onto the ferry and parked. Then the man turned a crank that pulled the ferry along a cable that stretched from one bank to the other. The moment the ramp touched ground on the opposite side, Charlie drove off the ferry and up the winding road.

"You act like you do this every day," Kit said.

"Because I do. I ride across with other workers," he replied. "We work all over the park. I'm going to show you our base camp."

The road wound up the hill, past farm after farm, some boasting herds of cattle and sheep, some with fields of towering corn, ripe for picking. Other farms looked hard-hit, their fields brown, their barns and houses crippled with age.

"Charlie," Aunt Millie asked, "what kind of work do you do here?"

"While one camp works below in the caves, constructing new stairs and paths, the other three camps work aboveground getting things ready for a national park."

"Doing what?" Kit asked.

"Planting trees. Stopping soil erosion from over-farming. Building new park buildings. And razing houses and barns."

"Raising?" Kit asked. "You mean building new ones?"

Charlie tilted his head, as if he didn't want to say. "Unfortunately, just the opposite. There are almost six hundred families who live on the land that will become the park. They are all going to have to clear out eventually. It's a slow process."

He gazed ahead, as if picturing every single family in the area. "We dismantle houses, barns, and outbuildings all over the park's fifty-three thousand acres," he said, his tone somber. "We take 'em down board by board and reuse everything we can in new structures around the park."

"Oh." Kit thought about her own comfortable house. What if someone forced her family out and then took it down board by board? She felt a pang under her ribs. A tinge of homesickness—and something else, too. *Empathy.* She remembered how narrowly her own family had escaped losing their home. Her heart went out to the hundreds of families in the area who wouldn't be as lucky.

Charlie slowed the truck to a crawl and pointed out his window. Beyond a line of barbed wire, a wide swath of scorched earth stretched to charred, leafless trees beyond. A single stone chimney rose up from a black heap that had clearly once been someone's home.

"What happened?" Kit asked.

"It was arson. Someone set fire to it," he said,

shifting the truck into a higher gear.

Kit looked back at the charred remains. "How do you know it was on purpose?"

"The firefighters found an empty turpentine can not far from the house. Anything doused in turpentine will burn like blazes."

"But why . . . ?" Kit wondered aloud.

"That's what I'd like to know. The family had already sold to the park and moved off their land. Our crew was about to start taking down buildings. Instead, we had to spread out over dozens of acres, clearing underbrush, putting out embers, and digging ditches so the fire wouldn't spread. Now we've still got to clear out all the debris. It's put us behind schedule, but that's not the worst of it. If the winds had been different, that fire easily could have spread to our camp."

Aunt Millie murmured, "Oh, dear."

Charlie kept his eyes on the road and his hands on the wheel. For a few moments, he didn't say a word. Then he glanced at Kit. "Don't worry, Kit. I'll be fine."

Kit chewed on the inside of her lip. How could she not worry? As much as she wanted to visit the cave, there was something else she wanted even more: to find out who was causing trouble and putting her brother at risk.

chapter 2

A Surprise at Camp

"HOME SWEET HOME," Charlie said as he drove under a sign that read "Maple Springs CCC Camp." An American flag flapped at the top of a wooden flagpole, as if greeting them. Charlie parked in a gravel lot under the shade of large oaks.

As they hiked in to the camp, Kit glanced at the many buildings. She drew a deep breath, half expecting to smell smoke even this far from the burned farm, but instead her nostrils filled with the fresh scent of new wood.

"Charlie," Kit said, "if that fire had spread here, these wooden buildings would go up in a flash!"

Charlie motioned for them to follow. "Let's not focus on that. Come and see the camp. The whole place is laid out like a military camp, with thirty guys to every barracks. We wear old army uniforms and each have a single trunk for our belongings."

Outside a building marked "Hospital," a young man sat on a bench. Crutches leaned against the wall behind him. He looked up from his open book and waved, a cigarette between two fingers. Kit waved back.

Charlie opened the door to the building marked "Recreation Hall" so Kit and Aunt Millie could peer inside. A few guys played pool, and another fellow worked behind a counter. "We can buy candy, sodas, and playing cards here," Charlie told Kit and Aunt Millie.

At the edge of camp, a group played baseball. *Crack!* The batter—a towering, red-haired young man with broad shoulders—connected with the ball and sent it flying toward the surrounding woods. Cheers rose up from the field. "Run, Big Josh! It's a homer!"

Charlie nodded toward the game. "Baseball. It's a favorite pastime here."

"And eating, I bet," Aunt Millie said, patting the picnic basket on her arm. "I packed lunch."

They found a picnic table near a red water pump. Kit's stomach growled as Aunt Millie set out a feast of cheese and salami sandwiches, sugar cookies, apples, and homemade pickles. But even as she filled her plate, Kit couldn't help thinking about Charlie's safety. Who had set the fire? And why?

As they finished lunch, Charlie's eyes lit up. "Hey, before I forget, I have something for you. I found a few arrowheads while I was digging trenches, and was told I could keep them. I want to send them back with you. I don't want to lose them. Wait here; they're in my barracks."

"Can we go with you?" Kit asked. "I want to see where you live."

The edges of Charlie's eyes crinkled in a smile. "Okay. But you two will have to wait outside," he said, forefinger raised, "until I see if anyone is inside sleeping or changing."

Like the other barracks, Charlie's was long and rectangular, with simple wooden steps leading inside. He tripped over a backpack draped with a pair of socks drying in the sun, then stepped in and pulled the door closed behind him. A moment later, the door swung open and he waved Kit and Aunt Millie inside. "The coast is clear."

Kit followed her brother between two rows of neatly made bunk beds and past a woodstove that sat halfway down the aisle. Charlie stopped at the bed just beyond the stove and patted the top bunk.

"Here's home. And here are my worldly possessions," he said with a laugh, squatting beside a metal footlocker on the floor. He took a small key from his pocket, unlocked the trunk, and lifted its lid. Suddenly his face went white. Springing up from the open trunk, a coiled snake tucked its copper-red head, ready to strike.

"Get back!" Charlie yelled.

A strangely sweet cucumber scent filled the air.

Kit scrambled back, bumping her head on the bunk opposite Charlie's. Aunt Millie stumbled, but righted herself. They all back-stepped carefully toward the door. In horror, Kit watched as the snake moved its arrowhead-shaped head and flicked its tongue. It spilled out of the trunk, its thick body crisscrossed with hourglass-shaped bands of gold and tan, and wound its way across the floorboards toward the far end of the barracks.

As soon as they were back outside, Charlie closed the door behind them. "Wait here, and don't let anyone go in. I've gotta get somebody who knows how to handle snakes."

Kit crossed her hands over her thudding heart, as if to keep it from leaping out. She scanned the ground nervously. If the snake could get into the barracks, it could certainly find its way out again. Then a new thought made her gulp in a big breath. The trunk had been locked. Which meant that someone must have put that snake in Charlie's trunk *on purpose.*

Before she could find the words to tell Charlie, he was dashing across the lawn toward the baseball game. In a flash he returned, breathless, with the tall redheaded batter at his side. Between breaths, Charlie said, "This is Big Josh. Josh, my sister Kit and my aunt Millie. Josh is from around here, so he knows how to handle copperheads."

Without seeming to rush, Big Josh disappeared into a shed, returned with a long forked stick, and headed inside the barracks. Kit heard the floorboards squeak and the sound of moving furniture. Then Big Josh appeared, holding the forked stick high. The snake's head was gripped in the V, its three-foot length flailing. "Well, look what I caught for dinner."

"You're not going to eat it, are you?" Charlie asked.

Big Josh eyed the writhing body. "Thought you might want to taste copperhead, you not being from these parts." He edged closer to Charlie with the snake held high.

"Hey, get that away from here," Charlie warned, as Kit and Aunt Millie stepped back.

"Aw, I'm just razzin' you." With a laugh, Big Josh headed toward the woods and soon lumbered back with an empty stick.

"Did you—?" Kit began.

"Nah," he replied. "I let it go. Them copperheads usually don't look for trouble. And they keep down the rodents. Did you catch that cucumber smell?"

"Yeah, weird," Kit said, keeping her distance. She wasn't sure she liked Big Josh's sense of humor.

"Copperheads give off that smell when they get startled. I guess it thought that trunk was home."

"But how did it get in my trunk?" Charlie pressed.

A twinkle danced at the corners of Big Josh's brown eyes, as his bushy eyebrows joined up in concern. "Somebody's idea of a prank, I bet," he said.

"Some prank!" Aunt Millie crossed her arms.

"A garter snake, that would be one thing," Charlie agreed. "But a copperhead?"

Big Josh wagged his head of thick red hair. "Aw, you know how some guys are. I could think of any number who might—"

"But what if it had bitten him?!" Kit interrupted.

"I'd be over there," Charlie said, pointing to the hospital. "One guy got bit in the ankle by a copperhead and his whole leg turned purple— swelled up like a melon."

"Did someone pull a prank on him, too?" Anger built under Kit's ribs—fiery hot—but she drew her lower lip between her teeth to keep from saying more.

"Nope," Big Josh answered with a smirk. "That guy found that one all on his own down the road, moving a wood pile."

With the snake gone, Charlie returned to his barracks for the arrowheads. "Now they're your responsibility," he said, putting them in Kit's outstretched hand.

As she tucked the bits of chiseled stone in her

pocket, she whispered, "Charlie, I think you should keep an eye on Big Josh."

He laughed. "Oh, Kit. He's a big puppy."

But as they walked back to the aging red truck, Kit found it hard to let her suspicions go. "He handles snakes as if he doesn't have a care in the world. If he could take the snake out of the barracks that easily, he could have been the one who put it in there in the first place."

"You are a born reporter, Kit," Charlie said as he tousled her hair. "But honestly, of all the guys here, he's the last person I'd worry about."

Kit climbed onto the truck's front seat, between her brother and Aunt Millie. As they bounced down the road, sunshine blinked between leafy patches of deep green and open expanses of fields and farms. Kit waved to everyone they passed: field-workers, an elderly couple rocking on a porch, three teenage boys walking along the road. In return, she received mostly scowls and stares.

Her chest tightened. "Charlie, practically nobody waves back."

"Yeah," he said, hands planted on the steering wheel. "Not everyone wants a national park. Folks get paid for their property, but that doesn't mean they *want* to sell. Some families have been passing on these places to the next generation for over a hundred years. I understand how they feel. Nobody wants to be forced from their home. But the government has the power to do it. It's a law called *eminent domain*."

"Why do the people have to leave?" Kit asked. "Isn't Mammoth Cave National Park going to be all underground?"

"Nope. It's the land aboveground, too."

Kit gathered her thoughts and exhaled. "So the fire and the snake could be the work of somebody who's angry . . . angry that their land is being turned into a park."

"Maybe," Charlie said. "Might be somebody's way of getting back at the government."

Kit's thoughts tangled into a knot. "Charlie, I'm glad you have a job here. But . . ." Her eyes filled with hot tears. "I can't bear the thought that someone is trying to hurt you. You should come home."

Charlie shot her a glance and half-chuckled, but Kit could tell he wasn't really laughing, just trying to make her feel better. "No," he said. "I'm not running away. I'm doing important work here. And you're here to have some fun. Still, I'm keeping my eyes open, and, while you're here, you should, too."

"I will," Kit replied. "That's a promise."

chapter 3

The Letter

AUNT MILLIE READ the sign aloud:
"'Thatcher Farm.' This is it!"

The truck slowed as Charlie downshifted and
turned at the wooden sign. "Oh, it's been so many
years!" Aunt Millie said as they followed the winding, gravel drive. "I hope Pearl recognizes me."

Around the last bend, trees gave way to wide
fields surrounding a two-story clapboard farmhouse,
a red barn on a stone foundation, and several
outbuildings. Dozens of sheep grazed a grassy slope.
In another field, crops grew thick and green, edged
by a row of tall sunflowers, their gold-rimmed brown
faces nodding in the afternoon sun. Chickens clucked
and pecked outside a chicken coop. A speckled
black-and-white rooster picked that very moment to

ruffle his feathers, tilt back his red crown, and crow. *Roo-roo-a-rooooooooo!*

"Hello to you, too!" Kit replied.

As they pulled up to the large farmhouse, a plump woman with two white braids dashed onto the front porch. Her apron fluttered over a lavender sundress. She pressed her palms to her cheeks, as if to hold down a runaway smile. "Millie!" she called, her arms wide and ready. "God sent you on wings!"

Aunt Millie jumped out of the passenger door and met her friend in a hug. "Oh, Pearl! You haven't changed a bit!"

"And you must be Kit and Charlie. I'm Miss Pearl," she said, adding, "Charlie, you'll stay for dinner."

"Is that an order, ma'am?" Charlie grinned.

"Sure is," Miss Pearl said, hands on her hips.

"I'll never turn down a home-cooked meal." Charlie gave Kit a wink, then grabbed the luggage and headed onto the porch steps.

"Now, I must tell y'all," Miss Pearl said, her voice dropping to a whisper as she opened the front door. "Gran-mammy—my husband Jesse's mother—took to bed some days ago. We've set her up downstairs in the sewing room, where it's easier to care for her."

They stepped in. A banister staircase loomed in the entry. From the right came the *tick-ticking* of a clock and a bright shaft of afternoon sunlight. "The living room," Miss Pearl said. Through the open door, Kit spotted a stone hearth, and a spinning wheel beside it. On either side of a velvet sofa, side tables held a violin and dulcimer, waiting to be played. Then Miss Pearl turned and motioned to the smaller, darker room to Kit's left, where soft, rhythmic snoring rose from beneath a mounded pink quilt.

Miss Pearl whispered, "I hope y'all won't mind sharing Gran-mammy's double bed upstairs."

"Not at all," Aunt Millie said. "And she can have her bed back the moment she starts feeling better."

Miss Pearl folded her hands together and brought

them under her chin. "Yes, let's hope. Bless your heart."

Later, Kit sat with Aunt Millie and Miss Pearl on the front porch. Miss Pearl told them that, of her seven children, only two now remained at home. "JJ's out working with the menfolk—you'll meet him at supper. That there's our Dorothy Ann," she said, waving toward a figure in the pasture who was riding a mule bareback near a flock of white sheep. "She just turned sixteen. I swear, if she had her way, she'd have been born a lamb. She loves those sheep."

Dorothy Ann waved back, dark curls draping her shoulders.

Before long, a horse-drawn wagon pulled into the driveway. "That'll be the men. Now we can eat," Miss Pearl said with relief.

Everyone gathered in the dining room, which was wallpapered with tiny blue flowers on a white background. Kit's stomach rumbled with hunger. The table brimmed with smoked ham, creamed peas, corn biscuits, and sliced cucumbers and tomatoes.

Kit sat across from Dorothy Ann, who glanced up with a shy smile. Next to Dorothy Ann sat her brother JJ, a good-looking seventeen-year-old whose auburn hair dipped toward one eye.

Mr. Thatcher, Miss Pearl's husband, a short, wiry man, finished a prayer of thanks, and everyone began passing plates. Charlie handed a plate of ham steaks to JJ, who stabbed a slice with the serving fork.

When a man with rusty-looking teeth and thin-ning gray hair stepped in from the kitchen, Miss Pearl introduced him. "This is our guest, Mr. Henry."

"Pleased to meet you. Sorry I'm late, ma'am," he said to Miss Pearl as he took the empty chair.

"And where do you live, Mr. Henry?" Aunt Millie asked.

"Lost my place a year ago," he said, meeting her eyes. "Home's at the next place yonder that'll have

me. In return for food and lodging, I make baskets—
the finest white oak baskets around—and repair
broken seats on cane chairs. I stay with folks for a bit,
then move on before I turn moldy."

Kit studied Mr. Henry. Back in Cincinnati, she'd
met boys and men who'd lost their jobs and homes
during the Depression. She'd also brought food
to some of the women and children living in the
makeshift hobo camps below the railroad bridge. But
unlike the hobos, who hopped on trains and traveled
from town to town in search of work, Mr. Henry
seemed content to stay in the area and take what
work he could find.

"We're honored to have you." Mr. Thatcher
nodded at Mr. Henry. "Got to count our blessings.
We haven't felt the boot of the Depression like some
folks. Here, with our orchard, cows, pigs, chickens,
and plenty of canned goods—thanks to Pearl—we're
never hungry."

"Our farm's a little pocket of heaven," Miss Pearl

added, tears suddenly filling her eyes. "Or it was, until the letter came." She pressed her napkin to her lips.

"Letter?" Aunt Millie asked.

Kit's ears perked up. Out of the corner of her eye, she noticed Charlie's gaze drop to his plate. He let out a soft breath.

"*The* letter. Arrived a week and a half ago." Miss Pearl held her shoulders back, but her voice wavered. "We've known since we sold the farm last year that we'd have to leave one day. But the letter from the park service was our final notice. It said we had twenty-one days to leave our property. This time it's an order."

"And go where?" Kit blurted.

Aunt Millie gave Kit's hand a squeeze, as if to say *leave this to the adults.*

Mr. Thatcher pushed back from the table. "I'm lookin' for a place here in Hart County, outside park boundaries. If I can find one. They've paid us fairly enough for our property, but money's no good if it can't replace what we're losing." Then he stepped out the kitchen door and was gone.

"My Jesse hasn't been taking it well," Miss Pearl said. "He's taken to walking nights when he should be sleeping. This farm has been in his family for generations. It's all he's ever known."

JJ spoke up. "Pappy's been knocking on every door beyond the park. It's not easy finding something close by when so many families are in the same bind."

"Oh, Pearl," Aunt Millie said, rising from the table and placing her hands on her friend's shoulders. "We came at the very worst time. We'll turn around and leave first thing in the morning. I'm just as sorry as an empty stringer of fish!"

"Millie," Miss Pearl said, standing and facing Aunt Millie, "I've known about the farm since before we invited you. I didn't tell you because I thought you wouldn't come down."

Kit couldn't hold herself back. "We leave here on the twenty-eighth of August. So that means you have to leave your farm the very next day?"

Miss Pearl nodded.

Aunt Millie's voice dropped to a whisper. "Pearl, we don't want to be a bother."

"Don't you dare turn tail, Millie. I couldn't wait to see you, and now that you're here, you simply can't up and leave. Y'hear?" She bowed her head, paused, and looked up again. "Besides, I pretended this day would never come. But now . . . I truly must start packing. I could use your help, if you wouldn't mind."

"Mind?" Aunt Millie said, as if waving away a pesky mosquito. "That's what friends are for!"

Dorothy Ann peered up from under her dark bangs. "On top of everything, Gran-mammy is ninety-three years old, y'all, and feeling poorly."

"Speaking of Gran-mammy," Miss Pearl said, "I'll see if she's ready for some dinner."

Dorothy Ann jumped up from her chair. "I'll go." She filled a plate with food, then headed toward the sewing room.

"That girl loves her gran-mammy," Miss Pearl said softly. "I love to sew like Gran-mammy, but those two are peas in a pod. Gran-mammy taught Dorothy Ann everything she knows about tending sheep, carding and dying wool, and spinning."

"I have experience helping elderly folks," Kit said. Back in Cincinnati, she'd helped Miss Mundis, her Uncle Hendrick's next-door neighbor, when she fell and needed extra care. And she continued to help Uncle Hendrick at his big house, even though he was the grumpiest person in the whole world. "I'm happy to help with Gran-mammy if I can."

"Thank you, Kit," Miss Pearl said with a warm glance. "We appreciate that kindly." She exhaled deeply before going on. "Right now I think the best medicine for us is some music. JJ, before Charlie returns to Maple Springs, will you play us a few tunes?"

JJ turned to his mother with a nod. "Yes, ma'am." But as he stood, eyes gray as storm clouds, he shot Charlie a glance.

Kit recognized that look. It was the same one she'd seen earlier in the day when she'd waved to people from the truck. No one had waved back. Their faces were grim, like tombstones etched with two words: *Go away!*

Kit speared the last bit of ham on her plate and chewed it without tasting it. She couldn't blame JJ or anyone else for not wanting to leave their home. But it wasn't Charlie's fault that this area had been chosen for a national park. No matter how angry people might be, it wasn't right to take out their feelings on the CCC workers, especially not on someone as good-hearted and hardworking as her brother!

While Aunt Millie and Miss Pearl washed the dishes, Kit carried a cup of chamomile tea to the sewing room for Gran-mammy.

"Oh, thank you," Dorothy Ann said, rising from the chair beside the twin bed. "Gran-mammy, we have a visitor, Kit Kittredge. She's the niece of Mammy's old friend Mildred. They're visiting for a spell. Look, Kit brought you a cup of tea."

Gran-mammy's pale green eyes were surrounded by dark circles. "Well, aren't you a dear," she said. "Where did you come from?"

"Cincinnati," Kit said, quickly adding, "ma'am."

"Here, Gran-mammy. Let me help you sit up," Dorothy Ann said, scooting an extra pillow behind her grandmother.

From the living room came bright, rapid fiddling.

"That's my grandson JJ," Gran-mammy said. "Comes from a long line of fiddlers, y'know."

Kit nodded politely.

"He's awful good with that fiddle. Just like Dorothy Ann with the wheel. She spins fleece into the loveliest yarn you ever did see."

Dorothy Ann's fair cheeks reddened. "I'm still learning," she admitted. She lifted the cup of tea to her grandmother's dry lips. "Here, Gran-mammy. Try a little? You need to get your strength back."

But Gran-mammy snorted and shooed the cup away. She pushed back white strands of hair on her nearly bald head. "Just leave it. Now you girls ske-daddle. I'm fine."

Dorothy Ann set the cup down on the side table. "All right. Dinner?"

"No, thanks," Gran-mammy said. "Maybe later." Her thin eyelids closed.

Kit followed Dorothy Ann across the foyer and toward the lively music in the living room. Just before entering, Dorothy Ann leaned into Kit. "Leaving here is hardest on Gran-mammy," she whispered. "She took to bed the day the letter arrived. She's been getting weaker ever since. Breaks my heart."

Kit whispered back, "I'm so sorry." It was all she could think to say.

In the living room, Dorothy Ann sat at her spinning wheel and pumped the treadle until it began to spin. Kit perched on a footstool and watched as Dorothy Ann took a fluff of wool from a basket and stretched and twisted it into a strand of yarn on the wheel. Kit had never thought before about where yarn came from. *Wool from sheep turned into yarn … yarn knitted into sweaters, hats, gloves, mittens, and scarves.* Kit tried to picture Gran-mammy as a young girl spinning yarn. Now her granddaughter carried on her tradition.

Kit glanced at Charlie and shared a smile. Sitting on the sofa, he leaned forward, elbows on his knees, clearly enjoying JJ's music.

Commanding everyone's attention, JJ stood fiddling beside the stone hearth, tapping out a beat with the toe of his boot. His sour mood seemed gone. With his instrument tucked under his chin, he moved his left hand up and down the frets as his right hand held the bow, flying over the strings. He played song after song, the music growing louder and faster until, with a flourish of his bow, he stopped.

Mr. Henry started clapping and everyone joined in. JJ bowed to his audience, his bow and fiddle extending like wings behind him.

After a moment, Charlie stood. "I guess I'd better be going so I return Joe's truck on time." He thanked the Thatchers for their hospitality and headed for the front door.

"Will I see you soon?" Kit asked.

"You can count on it," Charlie assured her.

When bedtime came, Kit was grateful to put on her familiar nightgown. She was more tired than she realized. What a long day it had been! She settled her head on the pillow beside Aunt Millie, who dropped quickly into sleep.

Kit lay awake, eyes open. A crescent moon rose and sent pale light into the bedroom. Kit suddenly missed Mother and Dad; her best friend, Ruthie; and her sweet dog, Grace, who often slept at the foot of Kit's bed. When Grace pressed her warm body against Kit's feet, sleep always came easily.

Time suddenly stretched like the long, endless steel rails she and Aunt Millie had traveled. Nine more days until they headed home? She swallowed hard, determined not to cry.

Her feelings didn't make any sense. She'd been so excited about this trip, about seeing Charlie, and the possibility of visiting a real cave. She loved spending time with Aunt Millie, and it had all sounded like such an adventure. But now Kit felt as if she didn't belong. She felt caught between two worlds: the one her brother was here to help build and the one—full of family farms like the Thatchers'—that was destined to be torn down.

She wished there was some way the Thatchers could stay on their farm.

Kit drew a deep, long breath. Then, like a quickly deflating balloon, she exhaled a sigh of worry. Things felt complicated—and yet they were simple: Families were being forced to make way for a national park. People were deeply upset. And Charlie was in danger, because whoever put a snake in his trunk and started a fire was still out there, ready to strike again.

chapter 4

Ghostly Warnings

THE NEXT MORNING, wanting to be help-ful, Kit brought a plate of scrambled eggs and but-tered biscuits to Gran-mammy. After her first bite of biscuit, however, Gran-mammy's hand went to her throat and she coughed and coughed. Kit raced back to the kitchen and returned with a glass of water. Gran-mammy took a sip and swallowed. "Much bet-ter. Thank you, sweetie."

After breakfast dishes, Kit helped Dorothy Ann feed chickens and collect eggs from the nesting boxes, something she knew all about from tending her small flock at home.

As Kit helped hang a basket of laundry to dry, Miss Pearl gave her a smile over the clothesline. "Thanks, Kit. You're a great help. But you're on

vacation," she added, fastening coveralls to the line
with wooden clips. "You should have a little fun
while you're here, too."

"I *am* having fun," Kit said, forcing a smile. She
wanted it to be true. But between worrying about
Charlie and doing chores in the sweltering heat, she
wasn't so sure.

The sun climbed high over the farm, and by mid-
afternoon it turned everything steamy, including
Kit. She sat on the porch, shucking corn in the shade
next to Aunt Millie, who was slicing cucumbers for
pickles. Droplets of sweat tickled Kit's back and clung
to her cotton blouse. She'd give anything to jump
into cool water. Even the sheep's water trough looked
inviting—almost.

Mr. Henry sat in a rocker at the far end of the
porch, weaving a basket from long strips of white
oak that were soaking in a pail of water. His rocker
creaked between pauses as he talked. "Before the
national park stepped in, I lived with my brother and

his family. Never had a wife or kids of my own, so taking a room with them suited me just fine—until he was forced off his land. He and his family headed west to start over. Not me. I wanted to stay."

"And so you did," Aunt Millie said, her knife flashing as disks of cucumber dropped into the bowl on her lap.

"Basketmaking is what I know," Mr. Henry said. "It's been passed down from my pappy's side of the family for generations. And now the CCC's wiping all that away, as if we never existed. God will surely punish the wicked. As in the Old Testament, He will bring down fire and brimstone, plagues, and any manner of serpents."

Fire? Serpents? To Kit, the words stung, as if Mr. Henry meant them to be hurtful.

"Mr. Henry, my brother works for the CCC," she said. "He isn't wicked. Are you saying that God will punish him for the work he's doing for the park and the CCC?"

Mr. Henry snorted in reply, as if the answer were obvious.

Kit turned toward Aunt Millie for support. "Charlie's doing as he's asked to do. He works hard. They plant trees and build trails. He makes a dollar a day and sends twenty-five dollars home every month to help our family. That can't be wicked, can it?"

"Of course not," Aunt Millie assured her. "But Mr. Henry was born and raised around here, and he has a right to his feelings."

With a cough and a loud clearing of his throat, Mr. Henry drew a strip of white oak from the bucket beside him and began adding another round to his basket.

"What kind of basket are you making now?" Aunt Millie asked warmly, as if smoothing out a wrinkled dress with an iron.

"A rucksack," Mr. Henry replied, "like this one here." He motioned to the tall, tightly woven tote beside his rocker. The hinged lid was flipped open over wide leather straps. A small brass key dangled from an unfastened lock at the front.

"What will it be used for?" Kit asked, admiring it.

"Well, whatever its owner wishes. Works for carrying all manner of things. Kindling, tools, small game."

A thought flashed through Kit's mind. "Could it carry snakes?" she asked casually.

Aunt Millie sent Kit a *don't-stir-up-trouble* look.

"Now why would anyone want to carry snakes?" Mr. Henry asked, leveling his pale-eyed gaze at Kit until she was forced to look away.

Aunt Millie came to Kit's defense. "It seems some-one put a snake in her brother Charlie's trunk in his barracks. I think that's what Kit was wondering about —just *how* it got there."

Kit concentrated on peeling back the leaves from another ear of corn.

"Well, no one's listening to us old-timers," Mr. Henry went on, as if he were continuing a conversation all by himself. "Blasted park is going to happen no matter what I say. But God will be the judge on Judgment Day—if someone doesn't take things into his own hands first!"

At his words, Kit met Aunt Millie's eyes.

Kit kept her thoughts to herself as she worked. Mr. Henry had lost his home. He'd been staying with the Thatchers a few weeks already—the same time frame of the recent troublemaking. And he was certainly angry.

Hoofbeats sounded on the driveway as Kit dropped the last ear of corn in the pot. She stepped off the porch toward the sound. Around the bend appeared two horses and one young rider. The boy's dark skin contrasted with the buff-colored coat of his horse.

"Hi. I'm Benny," he called out, bringing both horses to a stop. "This is Honey," he said, with a motion of his right hand and reins. In his other hand, he held the reins to a speckled gray horse, saddled and ready to ride. "And this is Cloud."

"I'm Kit, from Cincinnati," she called back. "Visiting the Thatchers with my aunt Millie."

"Miss Pearl asked if I might be your guide and show you a cave," said Benny.

Kit's heart lifted. Caving and horseback riding? It was more than she could have hoped for, but she hesitated. "I've never ridden a horse before," she told him.

"Cloud's gentle," Benny said. "You can pet him if you like."

Kit looked at the horse's soft brown eyes and ran her hand down the slope of his nose to his velvet-soft muzzle. "Hi, Cloud." But as Aunt Millie drew closer, Kit's enthusiasm dimmed. "I'm sorry," she said to Benny. "I can't afford much—actually, I can't pay anything for a guide, or a ride."

Miss Pearl had come outside and joined them. Now she spoke. "Kit, don't you worry about that. We and the Bransons barter all the time. I'll pay for

Benny's services today with a few dozen eggs." Miss Pearl turned to him. "Benny, you must promise to take it slow and easy with Kit today. I want her back in one piece. Y'hear?"

"Yes, ma'am," Benny replied, sliding off his mount. "My pappy always says that first, you have to keep your customers safe. Second, you want to keep them happy."

"He would know," Miss Pearl agreed. "Can you visit a cave and get back by six o'clock for dinner?"

Benny glanced at the sun. "Looks to be about three o'clock now. Yes, ma'am."

Miss Pearl turned to Kit. "You've done a good day's work already, Kit. Off with you now, and have yourself a good time. And if you bump into old Floyd, just tell him hello for me." She winked at Benny, but he didn't seem to notice as he helped Kit climb into Cloud's saddle and adjusted the stirrups.

"Your brakes are in your hands," he told Kit. "Just pull back and say 'whoa.' But if you ever find yourself on a runaway horse—"

"Runaway?" Kit asked.

Benny smiled. "Don't worry. It likely won't happen, but say we get startled by a bear, you want to know how to stop a frightened horse." He demonstrated by pulling one rein until Cloud turned his head toward the saddle. "Just like this. You pull one rein tight and he'll turn his head. He'll have to circle, and that will slow him down. Got it?"

Kit nodded, hoping for no bears.

It didn't take her long to settle into a rhythm in the saddle. With the balls of her feet in the stirrups, one hand on the saddle horn, and the other holding the knotted leather reins, Kit rode Cloud down the tree-shaded gravel road after Benny and Honey.

Kit didn't have to steer. Cloud followed willingly behind Honey's tail as they walked on the shoulder of the road. They cut left into the woods under a giant umbrella of tree cover.

At a small stream flowing between moss-covered

boulders, Honey picked her way carefully across. Cloud followed, but stopped midstream. Both horses stood still, their ears pointed straight ahead. Kit's heart gathered speed. She stared at the undergrowth ahead, looking for anything that might startle her horse: a black bear, snake, or bobcat.

Benny pointed left, just as two deer bounded into dense woods, their white tails waving high. Then, unconcerned, the horses lowered their heads and rode on.

Kit sensed Cloud relax beneath her. "Benny," she said. "I have a new plan. If we come across a snake or bear, I think I'd be safer on a runaway horse. At least I'd get away fast!"

Benny laughed.

They emerged from the woods at the edge of the vast, charred field she'd driven by earlier with Charlie. "My brother said someone set fire to this place."

Benny was silent for a few seconds. Finally he said, "That so?"

A freshly dug trench extended the length of the pasture. Kit could only imagine how hard Charlie and the other men had worked to stop the fire from spreading. "See, they dug trenches so the fire would burn itself out."

The horses stirred up a blanket of soot and ash as they rode past the remains of the house and chimney. "The Prescotts used to live here," Benny said. "Nice place. Two barns. Ten kids. I was friends with a couple of 'em. There was a river of tears when they said good-bye."

"How sad," Kit said. "Were they angry, too?"

"Who wouldn't be?" Benny replied.

Kit hesitated, then asked, "Do you think one of the Prescotts could have set the fire for revenge?"

Benny scratched an eyebrow. "Not likely. They cleared out two months ago. Haven't seen 'em around here since. Heard tell they drove all the way to California."

In the middle of the charred field and rubble from

the burned-down house, the stone chimney looked lonely. Kit tried to imagine the space around it filled with a rocking chair, a big family, a kitchen, a cat purring on the hearth ...

Honey snorted, and Cloud followed, as if the acrid smells were making their noses itch.

Kit and Benny rode on through leafless, inky trees. *A graveyard forest,* thought Kit, as ash clung to her clothes and nostrils. They rode down a slope and eventually back through trees untouched by fire. The air sweetened with each step. "Are we heading toward the river?" Kit guessed.

"Yes, ma'am."

"You can just call me Kit," she said to Benny's back.

"Okay, Kit," he agreed.

Benny stopped his mare beside a boulder and removed both horses' bridles, leaving their halters on, and tied them up to separate trees. Then he helped Kit off, saying, "Here's the cave. You ready?"

Kit looked around. She didn't see any gaping hole leading into the earth. "Where?"

"You'll see." Benny walked several yards toward the river and returned with a tall stalk. "It's a torch," he said. "I make 'em from cane stalks and keep a few here. Guides use them to tour the caves. Flashlights cost money. This way I get light for free." He pulled a small box of wooden matches from his pocket, lit one, and held it to the top of the stalk. The flames licked, rose, then settled into a small flame.

To Kit's surprise, the entrance to the cave was almost under her feet. Benny pushed away a few fallen stumps that covered its entrance, which plunged straight down into the ground. All Kit could see was the top of a flimsy-looking wooden ladder leading into darkness.

"I'm not sure—" she began, but Benny had started down the ladder, with one hand holding the torch. Kit watched him descend into the hole.

At the bottom, about ten feet down, the torch

illuminated his face. "Just go slowly," he called to her.

With a deep breath, Kit forced her feet onto the ladder rungs and began climbing down. "I thought we were going to the big entrance," she said as she lowered herself into the deepening cold. "You know, the one for tourists, the Historic Entrance."

"You have to pay a grown-up guide for that," he said. "Mammoth Cave is huge, with lots of caverns. This one here will never be a tourist cave, but that's why I like it. I think of it as my own cave."

When Kit's feet touched solid earth, she looked around. The cave walls expanded into a space as large as a classroom, with low ceilings. "How did you find this?" Kit asked.

"It's easy when you know what to look for," Benny said with apparent pride. "I come from a long line of guides. My family goes all the way back to the earliest cave explorers and guides around here. I grew up listening to cave stories since I can remember."

"So how did anyone first find the big cave?" Kit asked.

"There was a hole people wondered about," said Benny. "My great-great-grandpappy was ordered to go down it on a rope."

"Ordered? You mean someone made him?"

"Kit, he was born into a slave family. He was someone's property."

"Oh!" Kit said, shocked and embarrassed. "That's terrible."

Benny continued. "Guess he did as he was told. Probably scared witless at first to go down into some hole. But then, with a cane torch, he looked 'round and realized he was the first man of his time to see inside the big cave—the first to discover Mammoth Cave and explore its mystery and beauty!"

Kit had the feeling Benny never got tired of telling this story.

"He just got so he wanted to see more and more of the cave," Benny went on. "Every second he could, he went back to the cave, and he spent the rest of his life mapping out new routes and passages. And his son, and his son's son, kept up guiding. For years, the Branson cave guides were the most requested guides by wealthy tourists coming to see the caves."

Benny held the torch up and led Kit to the edges of the cave. Water *drip-drip-dripped* along cave walls and disappeared into cracks in the rock-strewn floor. Kit shivered, partly from the damp, cool air raising goose bumps on her skin, and partly from the mysteriousness of being underground.

"Ever find anything interesting down here?" she asked, staying close to the smoking torch and flickering light.

"A couple of Indian arrowheads," Benny said. "Means people have been discovering these caves for hundreds, maybe thousands of years."

Kit tried to imagine what people might have been doing in a cave so long ago. Maybe just what she and Benny were doing: exploring.

"Is your dad—I mean your pappy—still guiding?"
she asked Benny.

"Oh, he'll always explore caves. It's what he loves
most. But he might not always get paid to do it. Once
the park is up and running, only park rangers will
lead the tours."

"Couldn't he get hired by the park?"

Benny shrugged. "Maybe. He'd like to. Don't
know if the park'll hire Negroes to be guides. As
Pappy says, 'Sometimes people only see the color of
a man's skin instead of his skills.'" His eyes brimmed
suddenly, and he turned away. "Last week, we got
our letter. That's why I jumped at the chance to go for
a ride. The talk is pretty sad at my house."

"Twenty-one days till you have to leave?" Kit
asked softly.

Benny nodded. "The Thatchers are one week
ahead of us. But we're right in line after them to get
kicked off our land." His torch died away into red
embers, and Kit could barely make out Benny's face

until he blew on the torch, bringing it back to life again.

She swallowed. "Where will you go?"

He shook his head, then wiped his eyes with his shirtsleeve. "See, we're tenant farmers."

"Tenant farmers?" Kit repeated, not understanding.

"We pay rent to live on our farm and work the land," Benny explained. "We don't own the land, so we couldn't sell it to the park. The owner sold a while back. We've just stayed, waiting for that letter. We don't have anywhere to go, or any money to buy a place of our own."

"I'm sorry," Kit said.

For several moments they didn't say a word.

Drip, drip, drip.

Benny held the torch high. "That dripping? It's how the cave gets bigger. It's always changing. Drops of water wear away the stone and carry it off, bit by bit."

Kit looked up at the stone ceiling. Something dark and smaller than a teacup suddenly wiggled. She flinched and jumped back. "Oh my gosh, a bat!"

Benny shrugged. "That little fella isn't causing any harm. He lives here."

The brown bat hung upside down. It stretched its wings wide and drew them back in again. Then it yawned, revealing a tiny pink mouth, before it settled, motionless, another shadow on the cave ceiling.

Kit shivered involuntarily, glad the bat wasn't flying about her head.

Benny walked back toward the ladder and squinted up at the sky. "Guess we better get going if I'm going to have you back by six."

"First, safe," Kit said, laughing. "And second, happy, right?"

Benny broke into a smile. "Kit, you are exactly right."

Kit welcomed the climb up the ladder into the warm sunshine. Under towering trees and a wide blue sky, she drew a breath of sweet honeysuckle and stepped through long grass toward Cloud, who was dozing.

"Stop." Benny's voice was emotionless, but firm. "Don't move."

Kit froze.

"I don't want you to jump or scream. Just stay calm."

She eyed the ground. Then she spotted movement a yard away, between her and Cloud. A dark shape slithered almost unseen, as if a wisp of breeze had stirred a few blades of grass.

Suddenly the snake lifted its head, flattened, and flared its neck like a cobra, hissing.

Kit held her breath as Benny sprang forward and planted his boot on the snake. He reached down and snatched it up, his hand just below the snake's head, its jaws forced wide. The snake wiggled—a three-foot length of patchy tan and brown—and whipped its tail, but Benny held on.

"What is it?" Kit asked, her throat dry.

"Some folks call 'em puff adders or blow vipers," Benny told her. "It's just a hognose snake."

"Be careful," Kit said.

"It's not poisonous, but I was worried that if it startled you and the horses broke loose . . ." Benny laughed. "Well, we'd have an awfully long walk back." He walked a few yards down the slope and tossed the snake into a thicket.

Kit exhaled, relieved that it wasn't another copperhead. Still, as they trotted back home along a sandy path, worry crept back. Not about the snake, but about Benny himself.

She thought of the close call with the copperhead at Charlie's barracks. Just like Big Josh, Benny was awfully good at handling snakes. He was awfully good at lighting a torch on fire in the middle of nowhere, too. And he had plenty to be upset about. He'd been friends with two of the Prescott kids whose house had burned after they moved away.

And now his own family had to move.

There was as much reason to suspect Benny as there was to suspect Mr. Henry, Kit realized. The problem was, she really liked Benny.

Kit sat up straighter in the saddle, reminding herself not to be blinded by her feelings.

"Benny," she called, "somebody put a copperhead in my brother's trunk. He was lucky he didn't get bit."

"Yeah?" Benny said, glancing back briefly.

"I saw the way you took care of that hognose snake," Kit said to his back.

"Yeah, well, a copperhead is different. If I see one of those, I walk the other way. Better to avoid 'em."

"So, do you know who might be angry enough to start a fire at the Prescott farm and put a poisonous snake into Charlie's trunk?"

Benny drew his horse to a stop and pivoted toward her, his lips pressed together.

"Lots of folks around here are angry," he said, meeting her eyes. "Including me."

Kit waited. If he confessed, then what? Could she make him promise he would do no more harm?

"But I'll tell you who I think is spittin' angry and causin' trouble. Anytime things go wrong, we blame old Floyd."

Kit frowned. "Who?"

"Floyd Collins. That's what folks say around here."

"Who is he?" Suddenly Kit remembered what Miss Pearl had said just before they rode off. *If you bump into old Floyd, just tell him hello for me . . .* Was this the same Floyd?

"One of the most famous cave explorers of all time. He got famous when he was exploring Mammoth Cave and a boulder fell on his leg. A rescue worker finally reached him and was able to drop water and food down a hole. Folks came from all over the country and set up tents outside the cave entrance, almost like a circus."

"So is he a guide? Is he losing his job or his

land—or both? Is that why he's so angry?"

Benny shrugged. "Over time, plenty of folks say they've had their encounters with Floyd. I imagine he isn't happy about all the changes going on around here."

"Well, nobody has the right to put others' lives at risk," Kit said with conviction. "Somebody should talk to him."

"Can't," Benny said. "He died ten years ago."

chapter 5

Trust No One

FLOYD COLLINS WAS a *ghost?*

If you bump into old Floyd, just tell him hello for me, Miss Pearl had said. From Benny's story, it made sense that Floyd had become a legend. But did Miss Pearl believe in his ghost? Did Benny? Kit couldn't tell. Still, either way, blaming a dead man for all the trouble made her feel queasy. Despite the heat of the afternoon, Kit shivered. She didn't tend to believe in ghosts, but someone, living or dead, was putting her brother at risk.

Why would Benny try to blame the fire on a dead man? Kit was still pondering that question on Wednesday afternoon as she helped Miss Pearl and Aunt Millie

65

bake biscuits for a picnic that evening at Good Springs Church. While she measured a mountain of flour into a huge mixing bowl, it struck Kit that the picnic would be the perfect opportunity to search for answers. There would be lots of families at the church. She could ask around and see if anyone besides Benny was blaming Floyd for the trouble.

They piled into the back of the Thatchers' truck— all except Gran-mammy, who was feeling poorly; Dorothy Ann, who insisted on staying behind to care for her; and Mr. Henry, who left early on foot, saying he didn't care to ride in a horseless carriage. The truck bumped along a rutted road to a sturdy white clapboard building nestled among beech trees. Cicadas hummed as Kit carried a large basket of biscuits, still warm, to one of the picnic tables between the church and the cemetery.

Aunt Millie spread out a floral tablecloth. "You can set those biscuits right here, Kit."

As Kit did so, she couldn't take her eyes off the

headstones, large and small. It seemed strange to eat so close to a place where the dead were buried.

While women set up the tables, and the men clustered near the front steps of the church, Kit roamed through the tiny cemetery, hoping to spot a headstone with the name of Floyd Collins. Some stones looked new, with crisply etched letters. Others were so worn that she couldn't make out any dates or letters at all. Just like the stone walls of caves, she thought, headstones wore away with time. She strolled through the grass, past tombstone after tombstone, wondering who these men, women, and children had been, what kind of lives they'd lived. She filled her lungs with fresh air, grateful to be alive.

A young woman holding a pink-faced baby appeared at Kit's side.

Kit jumped, startled. "Oh, you scared me! I didn't see you before."

"I'm sorry," the woman said, rocking the baby in her arms. "My baby's fussy. Walking soothes him."

She swept her free hand toward the rows of tombstones. "If you're looking for someone, I'm the one to ask. I'm the pastor's daughter, so I grew up knowing every stone here."

"I'm curious about someone named Floyd Collins," Kit said. "Heard of him?"

The woman lifted the baby to her shoulder. "I was about your age when Floyd Collins died. He had quite a life. The whole country waited to see if he would be rescued from the cave in time. But you won't find him in this graveyard."

"Because he's a ghost?" Kit said.

The woman shrugged. "People believe what makes sense to them." She walked off, humming to her baby.

Kit felt even more confused about Floyd. Clearly he was a real person, but did the pastor's daughter think he was a real ghost?

When a bell rang with deep, low notes—*Bong! Bong! Bong!*—Kit joined Aunt Millie and the rest of the congregation near the food tables.

"Welcome, church family and friends!" began a man with hair as white as the pastor's collar he wore. "Let's bow our heads in prayer and ask our Heavenly Father's blessing on this gathering."

Kit couldn't keep from looking around through half-opened eyes. She didn't see Benny, but she did notice that Mr. Henry had joined the group in back. He bowed his head slightly, but his eyes darted nervously. When she met his sharp gaze, Kit flinched and closed her eyes.

While people took turns filling their plates from the serving table, Kit stood in line behind JJ. "I guess the Bransons don't attend this church," she whispered.

"They have their churches," he said, "and we have ours."

Kit was silent for a moment. She wondered, did God think people should worship separately based on the color of their skin? She doubted it.

"Same with schools," JJ went on. "The CCC camps here are separate, too. Aren't things separate in Cincinnati?"

"Yes," Kit said. "In some places." Still, she thought, it didn't seem right.

After dinner, everyone headed inside the church and sat on wooden pews. The congregation sang several hymns, their voices harmonizing with JJ's fiddle and a dulcimer played by a woman who cradled the instrument in her lap. The way JJ tossed the hair out of his eyes after every song and the way he smiled at two teenage girls in the front row made Kit wonder if his mind might be more on the big stage he dreamed of than on the meaning of the hymns he was playing.

The pastor's sermon was short, to Kit's relief, and was followed by another hymn. Aunt Millie stood tall and loudly sang all the verses to "Amazing Grace."

After the song, the pastor cleared his throat and glanced at Mr. Henry, who was sitting at the back of the church. "I've been asked to allow an extra minute with y'all before we depart. Mr. Henry?"

Mr. Henry stepped to the front and faced the congregation. His lips widened into an awkward smile, framing his bad teeth. "Folks and families of Good Springs, we are in a time of great upheaval. The national park has been pushing us from our homes, scattering us like lost sheep. I, too, lost a regular place to rest my head. And now I feel like John the Baptist, wandering in the wilderness, eating locusts and honey. I stay with those who open their doors to me. Wherever God sends me, I remind everyone that we must hold fast to the things that bind us. Our faith."

A few amens rose up from the around the church.

"Our families."

"Yes," several women agreed.

"And our traditions," Mr. Henry continued. "That's why God has pressed upon my heart this very day ..." He stopped, and everyone waited.

"If God truly wanted folks to move off their lands,

He could send a tornado," Mr. Henry went on. "But
He has not. *He wants us to remain here.* That's why we
must unite as one voice!" He motioned with both
arms for everyone to stand, and the congregation rose
as one.

"We must stand together and resist! We must take
back our lands that God has ordained to be ours!"
Now Mr. Henry was bellowing, his face growing
red as he shook his fist in the air. "This is not one
landowner's battle against the park. This is a spiritual
battle of light against darkness! God's righteous
people against the roaring fires of hell itself!"

The pastor moved alongside Mr. Henry, his head
slightly bowed. "Thank you, Brother Henry, for
sharing with us." Then he motioned for Mr. Henry
to return to his seat.

Mr. Henry's eyes flashed. "I was just getting
started." But the pastor didn't say another word until
Mr. Henry stepped away from the pulpit.

...

That evening, Kit sat on the front porch steps with Aunt Millie, watching the sun drop into glowing layers of amber and magenta. Fireflies flickered in the pasture as the shadows deepened. Crickets sang. From the woods, an owl called. *Whooo-whooo-who-whooooooo!*

Who indeed, thought Kit.

"Aunt Millie," Kit asked suddenly, "what did you think of Mr. Henry's outburst? He was trying awfully hard to get people riled up against the park."

"He's passionate," Aunt Mille agreed. "I'll give him that. Still, truth be told, he reminds me more of a door-to-door salesman than John the Baptist. He could be selling the purest goat soap in Kentucky, yet I wouldn't fully trust him. As the bard put it—"

"You mean Shakespeare," Kit guessed.

"That I do," Aunt Millie said with a smile. "He wrote, 'Love all, trust a few. Do wrong to none.'"

"Do wrong to none," Kit repeated. "Mr. Henry seems mad enough to do wrong."

"Feelings are one thing," Aunt Millie said. "Acting on them is quite another."

"Shakespeare again?" Kit asked.

"No, that one is all mine. But yes, someone could be taking his anger out on others."

"Someone like Mr. Henry."

Aunt Millie stood and pressed her forefinger to her lips. "We must not accuse anyone of anything without proof—"

Before Aunt Millie had finished speaking, a figure emerged silently from the shadows along the driveway, startling them. The figure was coming toward the Thatcher house. Kit couldn't help thinking of Floyd Collins, and she stood up quickly beside Aunt Millie. Kit squinted at the figure in the dusk, trying to make it out. As it drew closer, she could see that it had a hunchback.

"Oh, Mr. Henry!" Aunt Millie exclaimed. "Why, you certainly took us by surprise!"

Mr. Henry. Of course, Kit thought to herself. He'd

chosen to walk to church and now he was arriving home. Still, his emergence from the dark made her uneasy. Had he heard her accusation? She edged closer to Aunt Millie until their shoulders touched.

"Evening, ladies," said Mr. Henry, shifting the rucksack on his back. "I'm turning in." Then he headed toward the small handyman's cottage near the barn.

At the sound of a closing screen door, Kit whispered, "He carries that rucksack everywhere— like a turtle carrying its home wherever he goes."

"He's quiet, too," Aunt Millie replied. "He sure surprised us."

Kit frowned. "He comes and goes, moving from place to place . . . Why, Aunt Millie, he could easily have slipped into the CCC camp to plant that snake when no one was there."

Aunt Millie looked toward the cottage and was silent for a moment. "Well," she said finally, "I can't say it seems likely, but I have to admit it is possible."

Suddenly the night beyond the porch steps felt very dark. Was Mr. Henry turning in, as he said? Or did he plan to slip out later when everyone else was fast asleep?

The owl hooted again. *Whooo-whooo-who-whooooo?* Despite the warm air, Kit shuddered. "Come on, Aunt Millie," she said. "Let's go in."

chapter 6

Highly Flammable

WITH THE RISING sun, Kit dressed for chores and found JJ and Dorothy Ann heading out of the kitchen. "I'm ready to help," Kit said.

"Chicken chores or milking cows," JJ said. "Your choice."

"I'll start with what I know," Kit said. "Chickens."

Dorothy Ann handed her a metal bucket full of food scraps. "Here you go."

A few dozen hens and a big rooster clucked, pressing close to the bucket. "Buck, buck, buck!" Kit called, as she did with her own small flock. She scattered the mixture of carrot and cucumber peelings, crumbled eggshells, pork rinds, curdled milk, and apple cores. With satisfaction, the chickens cooed, clucked, and pecked.

Then Kit followed Dorothy Ann into the dim light of the chicken coop. Dorothy Ann grabbed two woven baskets from a hook and handed one to Kit. "You can check the nests on the right, and I'll check the left."

From straw-lined wooden boxes, Kit gathered an egg here, three eggs there. At the last low box, hidden by shadows, she reached in to check for eggs, but instead, her fingers met something warm and soft. It pecked the top of her hand.

Kit jumped back. "There's a hen! She scared me!"

With a chuckle, Dorothy Ann said, "Sorry, I forgot to warn you about our brood hen, First Lady."

"Named after Eleanor Roosevelt?" Kit ventured. Eleanor Roosevelt was famous for her persistence at helping those in need.

"That's right," Dorothy Ann said. "When she gets an idea in her head, she doesn't back down. Right now, this hen is bound and determined to stay on her eggs until they hatch out. She's so dedicated to staying on her nest that she barely eats or drinks."

"So," Kit began. "Do you make her get off her nest, or leave her be?"

"Better to leave her be, or she'll get ornery."

Back out in the sunshine, Kit counted the eggs in her basket. "Almost two dozen!"

Before returning to the house, Kit asked if she could watch JJ milk the cows.

"'Course you can," Dorothy Ann said. "I'll bring in your eggs."

Kit stepped inside the milk barn. Dust specks danced in a shaft of light from a small window just beneath the low ceiling. The light fell perfectly around the short wooden stool where JJ sat, humming as he worked the udders of a brown and white cow. A stream of milk pinged against the sides of the metal bucket.

"You have an audience," Kit said. "Hope you don't mind."

"Fine by me," JJ said, glancing over his shoulder

at her. "I'm almost done." When he finished, he reached down to pick up the two full buckets. As he leaned forward, something small fell to the barn floor from the top pocket of his shirt.

Kit reached for it. A book of matches. "Here," she said, handing it back to him. "You dropped these."

"Uh, thanks," JJ said awkwardly, shouldering the barn door open. "Listen, don't say anything, okay?"

It took Kit a moment to understand. "Oh, I see. You don't want your parents to know you smoke."

"I don't smoke! What makes you think that?" he said, quickly shoving the matches back in his pocket. A frown creased his forehead. "You go on now."

Heading back to the house, Kit puzzled over JJ's reaction. Was he always this prickly? Or was it only around her and Charlie?

When Kit returned to the house, the kitchen was brimming with heavenly smells: hot coffee, pancakes sizzling on the griddle, and bacon spattering in a skillet. Mr. Thatcher sat at the head of the kitchen table, his hands around a white mug of steaming coffee. Aunt Millie turned slices of bacon with a fork. Miss Pearl lifted pancakes to a platter with a spatula. "Morning, Kit," she said.

"Morning, Mrs. Thatcher," Kit said.

"Gran-mammy has her tea. After you wash up, how about you girls bring her some breakfast?" said Miss Pearl. "Then we'll all sit down to eat together."

When Kit and Dorothy Ann entered the sewing room, Gran-mammy's eyes were closed. Her tea sat untouched on the bedside table. She reminded Kit of the baby robin she'd once watched outside her window. In the early days, its featherless head and closed eyes appeared much too large for its body. With each passing day, the bird had grown bigger and stronger. But with each passing hour, Gran-mammy only seemed to shrink and grow weaker.

As Kit stood by, Dorothy Ann whispered, "Gran-mammy?" She set a tray of scrambled eggs and toast on the side table. Then she ran her fingertips across her grandmother's blanketed shoulder.

"Mmmm," came the reply. "Dorothy Ann, my sweet girl..."

"Yes, Gran-mammy?"

Kit's heart went out to Dorothy Ann. Not only was she going to lose her family's farm, but it appeared she was losing her grandmother, too.

"Eggs to pay for cave guiding," Miss Pearl said, handing Kit one of the egg baskets after breakfast. "Two dozen. Will you take these down the road to the Bransons?"

"Sure," Kit said. Basket on her arm, she headed out the back door and down the driveway.

Though it was only midmorning, the sun beat down on her shoulders and back. The air was humid, as thick as soft butter. Cicadas buzzed, filling the air with a deafening pulse. A frog hopped from one ditch to the other, crossing the gravel road in five hops. A hawk lifted from a wooden fence post, swooped down to the grass, and rose to the sky with a mouse in its talons, tail dangling. *Nature,* Kit thought, *is much simpler to understand than people.*

At the first gravel driveway beyond the Thatchers' farm, a wooden sign read "Famous Branson Cave Guides for Hire!" As Kit walked by the pasture, Honey and Cloud lifted their heads from grazing to look at her, then returned to munching green grass. Up ahead, the Branson farm consisted of two small houses and several outbuildings. Benny was in the yard, playing fetch with a large dog. He spotted Kit and waved. The dog barked and began trotting to Kit, its tail wagging furiously.

"Hi, Benny!" Kit called. "I have your eggs."

"Down, Bingo!" Benny shouted as the dog jumped up, setting its paws on Kit's chest.

Kit's feet slipped out from under her. As she lost her balance, she tried desperately to hang on to the egg basket. "Oh no!" She wheeled her arms to regain her balance, but the weight of the basket, and a second happy pounce by Bingo, doomed her. She fell backward onto the gravel, and the basket fell in a thud next to her. She felt pain in her elbow, but nothing could be worse than losing the *whole* basket of eggs.

Benny grabbed her hand. "Here," he said, pulling her to her feet. "You okay, Kit?"

Kit bit her lower lip. The eggs were a puddle of yolks, whites, and cracked shells. Only two unbroken eggs remained. "What a mess!"

Tail and body wagging, Bingo bent his head to the eggs and began lapping them up.

"Well, there's your answer to the mess," Benny said. "But a few broken eggs—"

"Almost two dozen!" Kit moaned.

Benny shrugged. "Well, even that seems a pretty small thing compared to what's going on around here these days."

"I owe you another basket," Kit promised him.

"Sure, when you can. That's fair," said Benny. "Now, I think you're bleeding. Come on in, and let's get that arm cleaned up."

After Benny made hasty introductions, his mother took charge. A tall woman with striking cheekbones and hair pulled into a bun, Mrs. Branson said, "Now Kit, you sit here on the porch swing. And Benny, one of the pigs got out. See if you can round it up while I help Kit here."

"Yes, ma'am." Benny set off toward the outbuildings and pens.

Soon Mrs. Branson returned with a washbasin of warm water and cleaned Kit's wound. After the bleeding stopped, she applied a pungent-smelling salve.

Kit wrinkled her nose. "It sure smells strong."

Mrs. Branson nodded. "It's made from lard and turpentine. That's the turpentine you're smelling."

"Turpentine?" Kit said. "Isn't that the stuff that starts fires?"

"Well, yes, it's highly flammable," said Mrs. Branson, "but it's not for fires. The oil comes from certain pine trees, and we use it for all kinds of things, like paint thinner and furniture polish, and even medicine—easing achy joints or infection of the lungs. I always keep a good supply in my storeroom to use in remedies. I have a whole collection of remedies," she added. "Now, let me wrap this for you, to keep it clean."

What was it Charlie had said about the Prescott farm? *The firefighters found an empty turpentine can not far from the house . . .*

Kit bit her lip. If Mrs. Branson kept lots of turpentine on hand, would she notice if a can went missing?

As Mrs. Branson finished wrapping Kit's arm with a strip of light blue fabric, Kit met her eyes. "I'm really curious about your remedies. Could I see your storeroom?"

Mrs. Branson smiled, as if pleased that Kit was

interested. "Of course. This way." She led Kit outside
to a small shed, just big enough for one person to step
into. Bundles of dried herbs hung overhead. Pickling
jars with colorful ingredients lined the shelves.
Beneath, several cans of turpentine sat on the floor.

"So interesting!" Kit exclaimed. "Who needs a
drugstore when you have all these remedies?" She
forced herself to look around at everything and not
only at the cans of turpentine. She hated suspecting
Benny, but she couldn't deny that he had access to
plenty of fire-starting materials.

"Thank you, Mrs. Branson," Kit said, stepping
back outside. "And I'm really sorry about the eggs."

Mrs. Branson laughed. "No, *I'm* sorry. That Bingo,
he's still a big puppy. I apologize for his rude behav-
ior! Do you know the song?"

"B-I-N-G-O?" Kit guessed, as they stepped back
onto the front porch. "We used to sing that at school."

"Yes, it's a good spelling song for little ones," said
Mrs. Branson.

"Kit!" Benny ran up the porch steps, carrying two squirming kittens in his arms—one dark gray and one calico.

"Oh!" Kit exclaimed. Seeing the kittens pushed the questions about Benny from her mind.

"There's seven," Benny said, motioning with his head toward the barn. "But two is all I could carry. Want to hold one?" He hopped onto the wide porch swing.

Kit joined him on the swing, and he handed her a soft gray ball of fur. It mewed as Kit held it up and peered into its light blue eyes. "Aren't you a sweetie?" she murmured.

For several minutes, Kit and Benny swayed in the swing, cuddling the kittens.

"They need names," Benny said, holding the calico to his chest.

The gray kitten nosed Kit's cheek, then licked, its tongue warm and scratchy. Kit laughed and tucked the kitten under her chin. She hadn't started the day with any wish for a kitten, but now, how she wished this soft, snuggly little bundle could be hers! She reminded herself that it was a long train ride to Cincinnati. And she doubted her parents would agree to a kitten. Anyway, she was supposed to be focusing on Charlie's safety, not on little balls of fluff! Still, she thought, it couldn't hurt just to name them ... "How about Smoky for this one?"

"Yeah, that's good," Benny said. "And this one?"

The calico purred more loudly, as if with anticipation of a name.

"It's as if someone took paint," said Kit. "Brown, white, black, gray, and gold paint—and splattered him all over."

Benny laughed. "It's all mixed together," he said, petting the calico kitten. "How about Stew?"

"No!" Kit said. "You can't possibly call a kitten Stew. It sounds like he's about to be cooked!"

"Yeah, you're right," said Benny.

Kit thought of Aunt Millie and her quotations.

"I know. How about Shakespeare?"

"Shakespeare? Why Shakespeare?"

"My Aunt Millie loves Shakespeare. She says he wrote about everything under the rainbow—and, well, look at this little fellow. He's a rainbow of cat colors."

Before long, Kit knew it was time to head back. "I'd better go," she said, handing Smoky back to Benny and picking up her empty basket.

"Want to take these two with you?" Benny asked.

"Want to? Yes, I would love to, but I can't."

Shakespeare tried to climb from Benny's shoulder to his head, while Smoky tried to twist out of his arms. "They need homes." Benny sounded pleading. "But when folks don't know if they'll have a place to call home, they don't want a kitten . . ." His voice trailed off, ending on a note of anger. There was a long pause before he spoke again. "No wonder people are hoppin' mad. Wouldn't surprise me if old Floyd didn't set something else on fire."

Kit couldn't help picturing the cans of turpentine in the well-stocked storage shed.

"Benny—" she hesitated, then took a deep breath and said what was on her mind. "My brother says a turpentine can was found at the Prescott farm that burned. A ghost wouldn't need turpentine to start a fire. "But a person might." She looked straight at Benny.

"Kit, you don't have to believe in Floyd," Benny said, meeting her gaze. "But I do. Strange things happen in the cave. A banging of rock against rock when you're so deep underground that there isn't sound. Someone grabbing your arm from behind, then you turn and look and nobody's there. Things a ghost would do."

"Have things like that happened to you?"

"Well, no, but it's happened to others. And they say sometimes a voice calls out, 'Wait!' or 'Help!' but then no one is there."

"Benny," Kit said, "I bet cave guides tell ghost

stories to entertain tourists. You know, to make the tours more exciting. And I bet someone is blaming something on Floyd that a real live person is responsible for. If you didn't see Floyd set the fire, how can you say it's so?"

"You're not from around here, Kit," said Benny, as if that explained it. "I am."

Frustrated by his reply, Kit picked up her empty basket. "I think I'd better go now."

As soon as she was out of view of the Bransons' house, Kit started whistling the tune to "Bingo." Ghost or no ghost, whistling kept her from imagining someone hiding behind every beech, poplar, and pawpaw tree she passed.

At the sign for the Thatchers' farm, she stopped whistling as a cold realization hit her. Benny hadn't acted a bit surprised when she'd mentioned the turpentine can. Maybe all the local people knew it had been found at the fire.

Or maybe Benny knew about it because he'd dropped it when he fled the scene.

She kicked a stone and sent it flying ahead of her down the Thatchers' driveway. She'd hoped to get the truth from Benny, but the only thing she'd learned was that Benny really believed in the ghost of Floyd Collins. Or, maybe, that he was incredibly good at distracting her from her suspicions. Because every time he brought up Floyd Collins, Kit realized, he'd taken the attention off himself.

chapter 7

Wounds New and Old

KIT FOUND MISS Pearl and Aunt Millie in the kitchen lifting pickle jars from a huge, steaming pot of water. The first thing Kit did was tell them about the broken eggs.

"Well," Miss Pearl said. "They say don't cry over spilt milk—guess that's the same for eggs, too. Looks like you took a bump."

Kit nodded at her bandaged elbow. "It will be fine. Mrs. Branson put some homemade salve on it."

"Oh, she's a fountain of wisdom when it comes to herbal remedies. I'm sure it will heal up fast. As to eggs, you'll have enough in a few days for the Bransons."

"Miss Pearl," Kit said, "Benny showed me a couple of kittens that need homes. They're adorable!

Think you could use a few extra mousers?"

Miss Pearl glanced around her kitchen, which was crowded with half-packed boxes. "What with moving, Kit, I dare not add any more critters to the chaos. Besides, we have one cat already."

Kit tried the idea of kittens on Aunt Millie next.

"You named one of them Shakespeare?" Aunt Millie said. She tousled Kit's hair. "Are you trying to soften me up to take one home?"

"Could you? Could we?" Kit pleaded.

"I can't imagine a long train ride is a good idea for two little kittens," Aunt Millie said in answer, before returning to canning pickles with Miss Pearl.

On the Thatcher farm, evenings followed a cozy routine. After the supper dishes were dried and put away, the kitchen floor swept, and Gran-mammy tucked in for the night, everyone gathered on the porch.

JJ took a wide stance, tucked his fiddle under his chin, and played a slow tune. Miss Pearl played the dulcimer on her lap, stroking its long strings with a pick. For a song or two, Mr. Thatcher hummed along, but soon he took to singing, his voice comforting and sweet as maple syrup. Aunt Millie joined in, harmonizing. Kit helped Dorothy Ann card wool and sang along, too, when she knew the words.

As Mr. Henry worked at repairing the seat of one of the Thatchers' chairs, he spoke up between songs. "What's going on around here is like what happens to a chair. You sit in it day after day for years. It's wearing out, but you don't notice it. Until one day . . ." He stomped one foot on the porch floor. "It breaks!"

His last two words hung in the air like a thunderclap.

"At least with a chair, it can be fixed by someone like you," Aunt Millie said, as if trying to soothe his foul mood.

"Humph!" he snorted.

Mr. Thatcher lit a pipe and drew on it until it sent up a sliver of smoke. "Mr. Henry," he said. It wasn't the start of a question. It was a two-word scolding, a reminder for Mr. Henry to be polite. Then, pipe to his lips, Mr. Thatcher cupped the bowl in his right hand and puffed, his gaze on the sheep pasture beyond.

Dorothy Ann looked up as she gathered tufts of rough wool from her basket to be carded. "I never want to leave. They say if cows aren't happy, they'll stop giving milk. I know my sheep are happy here, because their coats were thicker than ever when we sheared them this spring . . . and so many lambs this year!"

"If everyone leaves," Miss Pearl said, "I wonder who will be left to pass on the crafts, the stories, the remedies and recipes?"

"Folks will take what they know with them wherever they go," JJ said. "My music runs through my veins. Some of us will just follow our dreams farther away."

"JJ, you sound like you *want* to leave," Dorothy Ann said.

"I do and I don't," JJ replied. "What I know for sure is we're running out of time, and we can't just sit here and gripe about it."

Dorothy Ann piped up, her voice tight. "Well, I'll gripe all I want, thank you very much. I think the idea of moving is what sent Gran-mammy to bed. She's been goin' downhill since the day the letter arrived. It 'bout killed her then and there. I—"

"It's not that I *want* us to lose this farm!" JJ cut in, his voice raised. "That's the last thing I want. Thatchers settled here before the Civil War. This place has made us who we are! I'm angry. More than I can put into words!" He looked around from face to face, his chest rising and falling. "Moving pains me something awful. I've known for some time that I need to go to Nashville for my music—but I always figured I'd come *home* again."

Miss Pearl spoke up, her voice on the edge of

tears. "This land is in our bones. Babies birthed here. Loved ones died here. But JJ's right. We have to face what's coming."

For several minutes, everyone kept their thoughts to themselves. No one played or sang—or argued, to Kit's relief.

Leaning against the porch post, JJ glanced at Kit and winked, as if reminding her about the matches he'd dropped earlier: *Don't say anything.* Then he put the fiddle back under his chin. Forelock hanging over one eye, his expression was one of complete focus as his fingers and bow flew over the strings with the whir of hummingbird wings. Kit felt JJ's emotions— anger, passion, impatience—surge through his music.

When JJ finished playing, Mr. Thatcher rose from his chair, stepped off the porch, and headed for his lanky black horse Dixie, who was tied at the hitching post with her muzzle tucked into a feedbag. Mr. Thatcher removed the feedbag, tossed it into the back of the wagon, climbed up, and gathered the driving reins. His back straight as a broomstick, he set off.

Kit watched as Mr. Thatcher disappeared around the bend. "He doesn't talk much," she said, drawing tufts of wool between the carding teeth.

"Never has," Miss Pearl agreed. "He's terribly upset. But then, this is a difficult time for us all."

JJ put his fiddle back in its case on the floor, snapped the lid shut, then strode off toward the kitchen. The back door banged behind him.

Miss Pearl drew one long, deep breath and then exhaled loudly. "Sun's not all the way down yet. We need to get back to our packin'."

After Kit helped Dorothy Ann empty a linen cupboard of dishcloths, tablecloths, and napkins into flour sacks, they headed onto the back porch with glasses of sweet tea. The sun had set, and darkness was settling in.

"Want to catch fireflies?" Dorothy Ann asked as tiny lights flicked on and off in the dusk.

"Sure, but what about snakes?" asked Kit. "My

brother found a copperhead in his trunk at his work camp. Now I'm a little nervous about where I step."

"I didn't know about that," Dorothy Ann replied. "When?"

"The day we arrived," Kit told her. "I wonder if whoever put it there is the same person who started the fire at the Prescott place."

Dorothy Ann raised her eyebrows. "What does your brother think?"

Kit shrugged. "He's being watchful. And so am I."

"Well, at night you don't need to worry about snakes," Dorothy Ann told her. "They find a dark, cozy place to hide away and sleep." She smiled at Kit. "Come on, let's catch us some lightning bugs."

With empty mason jars in one hand and lids in the other, Kit and Dorothy Ann raced around the yard after blinking lights. "Caught one!" Kit called.

"Me too!" Dorothy Ann called back.

It was like catching tiny sparks of fire, thought Kit. She followed one firefly to the front of Mr. Henry's darkened cottage, then darted after the blinking light around the building's corner—and nearly ran headlong into a red ember at face level.

"Hey," a low voice said.

Kit nearly jumped out of her skin. "Oh!" In a flash, she took in the silhouette and breathed in cigarette smoke. It was JJ.

"You said you didn't smoke," Kit said.

"I couldn't have you telling my parents, could I? You won't say anything, will you?"

A firefly lit up between them. Kit drew the cover and jar together, trapping it inside. Then she turned away.

"Will you?" he whispered.

"No," Kit told him. She couldn't help feeling a little annoyed. He thought she was such a tattletale that he'd lied to her?

"Promise?"

"Sure, I promise." Kit bolted across the grass toward the farmhouse lights, her heart still pounding from the startle JJ had given her.

By the time she reached the back porch, where Dorothy Ann waited, she already regretted her promise. Hadn't JJ just declared in the parlor that they needed to stop talking and take action? *We can't just sit here and gripe about it,* he'd said. JJ seemed as angry as Mr. Henry, thought Kit, even if he showed it differently. And hadn't he lied to her about smoking?

Kit wondered what else he might be lying about. Some people, after all, were experts at lying, and she didn't know JJ well enough to know what kind of liar he might be. Was he just an occasional "white lie" sort, or the kind who might lie about dangerous things, like starting fires?

"How many did you catch?" asked Dorothy Ann.

The girls held their jars up and counted. Kit had caught seven to Dorothy Ann's nine.

"Let's show these to Gran-mammy," suggested Kit. "They might cheer her up."

In the sewing room, Gran-mammy sat up in bed

against pillows, her eyes closed.

"Gran-mammy," Dorothy Ann said. She held her jar behind her back, and Kit did the same. "We have a surprise for you."

Gran-mammy opened her eyes and lifted her head from the pillow. "I always like surprises. Is it my birthday?"

"No, but we can pretend. Look!"

Kit and Dorothy Ann held their jars close.

A smile stretched across Gran-mammy's face. Tears formed at the edges of her pale eyes and rolled down her cheeks. "Fireflies," she whispered. "I used to catch them as a little girl. Oh, thank you!" Then with a sigh, her head fell back against the pillow, as if that little effort had been too much. "I want to sleep now, girls."

"Here," Dorothy Ann said, handing her jar to Kit. "Let me help get a few pillows out from behind you."

Soon Gran-mammy was breathing slowly, her body looking small underneath the covers.

Kit and Dorothy Ann tiptoed to the kitchen. "I like a snack before bed," Dorothy Ann said. "How 'bout you?"

"Okay," said Kit.

Dorothy Ann unwrapped the cloth towel protecting a loaf of bread and cut two thick slices. "I've been trying to get Gran-mammy to smile for weeks now, and all it took was catching a few fireflies."

Kit grinned. While Dorothy Ann slathered butter and jam on slices of bread, she filled two glasses with milk. She handed one to Dorothy Ann. "I wish it were as easy to catch the person who started the fire and planted that snake in my brother's trunk. I'm worried he'll strike again soon."

Dorothy Ann met her gaze. "Think it's the same person, Kit? There's plenty of upset folks around here."

Kit wondered if *here* meant under the Thatcher roof or everyone living within the park boundaries. Maybe both.

chapter 8

Stirrings Aboveground

KIT WOKE TO a light patter on the slanted roof above her head. At home, she loved typing out stories in her attic bedroom during a good downpour. Now the rain made her a little homesick. Before following Aunt Millie down to breakfast, she found her satchel, pulled out her notebook and pencil, and decided to get the words in her head down on paper.

Home. There is no word more comforting.

Home. A cozy blanket you wrap around you.

Home.

My home is in Cincinnati. It's a big, rambling house. But it's so much more than a house. It's the people in the house that make a home.

She paused. She'd never thought about home much until Dad lost his job at the car dealership. If they'd missed making a monthly mortgage payment, Kit knew, they would have been out on the street, homeless. Her heart went out to the Thatchers, the Bransons, and everyone else in the Mammoth Cave area. No matter the reason, no one deserved to be forced from their home.

She wrote:

Home. It's where family gathers.

The word—*family*—suddenly stuck in her throat. Her family would be forever changed if something terrible happened to Charlie. She needed to tell him what she'd learned—about Benny and the turpentine, and JJ, and Mr. Henry—and ask him what to do. Determined to get to the CCC camp, she put away her pencil and notebook and dressed for chores. Maybe she could ask Mr. Thatcher to drop her by the CCC camp, she thought as she headed downstairs toward the rising scent of coffee, sizzling bacon, eggs, and grits.

The rain was short-lived. The sun popped out

as Kit and Dorothy Ann fed the chickens, who squawked at the girls' tardiness when they entered the coop. First Lady tried to peck Kit as she gathered nearby eggs. "Don't worry," Kit murmured to the hen. "I'm not going to disturb you."

Her egg basket full, Kit gazed out the door of the coop to see Mr. Thatcher heading off, slapping the reins across Dixie's rump as the horse pulled the wagon forward. *Shoot*, thought Kit—she hadn't had a chance to ask him for a ride.

By midmorning, the sun was scorching and the air was as wet as a washrag. As Kit helped with chores, sweat beaded up on her forehead and dripped down her spine. She swept the porch. *Sweat*. She helped hang laundry on the clothesline. *Sweat*. She fanned Gran-mammy with a fan made from an old newspaper. *Sweat*.

Drinking sweet tea with Aunt Millie and Miss Pearl in the shade on the porch after lunch, Kit was surprised to see Benny ride up on Honey, his bare feet dangling from his cutoff jeans. He led Cloud, who wore a saddle.

"Time for a swim," he called out to Kit. "Want to join me?"

Kit jumped up. She couldn't help feeling happy to see Benny, despite the fact that his name was on her growing list of suspects.

Still, she reasoned, riding Cloud was a way to get to the CCC camp. "May I go?" Kit asked Aunt Millie.

"Fine by me," Aunt Millie said. "I know you're a good swimmer."

"There's a current," Miss Pearl added, "so stay where it's shallow and you can keep your footing."

Kit raced inside and returned wearing a swimsuit under a pair of Charlie's old overalls. By the time she pulled herself up into the saddle and settled her feet into the stirrups, she had to wipe stinging sweat from her eyes. A swim would feel awfully good, Kit thought, but there was work to do first. She wanted to see Charlie . . . and she wanted to talk to Big Josh, who was also on her list of suspects.

When they rounded a bend, out of view of the Thatchers' farm, Kit said, "Can we stop by the CCC camp first and visit my brother?"

Up ahead of her on Honey, Benny was silent. Kit wondered if he hadn't heard her.

Finally he said, "I'm not a big fan of the crews who raze homes around here."

"My brother's a good guy," Kit said. "He's just doing his job, like anyone else."

"Either way, he'll be working until five or so," Benny said. "That's when they return to the camp. I see 'em roll by in trucks every day."

"Okay," Kit said. "We'll swim first, then visit."

When they reached the base of the valley, the riverbed opened into grassy patches. A kestrel hawk screeched as it flew over the river beyond. Benny tied the horses to a couple of trees. Then he led Kit down a narrow path to the river, stopping at a massive tree that leaned over the embankment. Water shimmered beyond through leafy branches.

Benny unfastened a rope secured to a nail on the tree. A large knot held a short wooden board with a hole in its center. Straddling the board, he held the rope with both hands. "Here goes!"

He pushed off the bank and sailed out, beyond the tree's wide limbs and over the Green River, then reversed motion and swung back again to the green shadows beneath the overhanging tree and back to the bank. He landed on bare feet.

"Woo-hoo!" He beamed at Kit, then pushed off again. This time, as the rope reached the end of its arc, Benny let go, dropped to the slow-moving river, and disappeared. Then he surfaced with a broad smile and dog-paddled to shore.

Kit gripped the rope, swung her legs over the wooden seat, and sailed out over the water. For a few terrifying seconds, she forgot about Charlie and about solving the mystery. She fell with a shriek and went under with a *ka-sploosh!* Her feet quickly found the sandy bottom, and she pushed through the water to shore, feeling refreshed.

Soggy, but much cooler, Kit rode behind Benny under the camp sign at Maple Springs. The American flag flapped overhead. Two rabbits bounded away. As the sound of wheels approached, Kit and Benny stopped their horses at the grassy entrance. Pickups brimming with workers were returning in a caravan to camp, just as Benny had predicted.

Dust and sweat covered the workers' faces after a full day's work, but many smiled and waved at Kit and Benny. Kit waved back. She noticed Benny didn't.

"You could act a *little* friendly," Kit suggested.

"Could," he muttered. "But I won't."

When the last vehicle passed, Benny slid off Honey's back. "You ride in, Kit. See your brother. I'll wait here."

Without protest, Kit nodded and rode Cloud

past the parking area and down the camp road. The moment she rounded the bend, out of sight of Honey, Cloud whinnied and slowed. Honey called back, high and frantic. Cloud stopped. Kit wasn't sure she could make a horse do something it didn't care to do, but she knew she should try. When Cloud wouldn't budge, she applied more pressure. First with her legs, and then with her heels. This time, Cloud took a step, then another.

With a little encouragement, Cloud picked up his pace again. At the first building, the camp hospital, two men headed toward the door. One towered and had to be Big Josh. The other—

"Charlie?" Kit called.

He stopped midway through the door and turned. "Kit! What're you doing here? And riding a horse?"

Big Josh smiled. "Hi, Kit."

"Looks like you went for a swim," Charlie said.

"I did. With a neighbor boy, Benny Branson. He's

waiting over at the entrance with his horse."

Then she noticed a soiled cloth tied around Charlie's right hand. "Did you get hurt?"

"It's nothing. A slight burn. I'll get some ointment and be good as new."

"What happened?" Kit urged Cloud closer and stopped just outside the wooden steps.

"Welding," Charlie said. "We were working on trail railings down in the cave."

"Happens to all of us," Big Josh said. He held up his large hands as proof. A few fingertips on each hand showed red spots still healing.

"I'll just be a minute," Charlie said as he disappeared inside the infirmary.

Kit eyed the burns on Big Josh's hands. It struck her that he might not have gotten them the way he claimed. "Josh," she said. "You're from around here, Charlie said. Is your family in the park boundaries? Will they have to move, too?"

A shadow passed across Big Josh's eyes, and his

thick eyebrows met above them. "Unfortunately." He gave her a simple nod, his expression serious, then he strode off toward the trees in the direction of a building Kit guessed was an outhouse.

Cloud pawed at the ground. "We'll go soon," Kit said, but the horse kept pawing. Kit tried loosening the reins. Immediately, Cloud lowered his head to the grass and grazed.

Several minutes later, Charlie stepped back outside, sporting a dazzling white cloth bandage. "Doc says I'll be fine." In his fingers he carried a few sheets of paper stapled in the corner. "I grabbed a copy of our camp newspaper." He handed it up to her. "Thought you might get a kick out of it."

Kit studied the camp paper. It was fancier and longer than the small newspaper she wrote and typed up at home, but she felt a kinship with whoever had put it together. She flipped quickly through the pages. Statistics from camp baseball games. A few jokes. Bits of news about CCC progress

on the park. A listing of movies at the Whoopee
Theater. "You get to go to movies at a theater?" Kit
asked with a smile. "I thought it was all work here
at the CCC . . ." She trailed off as the smell of smoke
tickled her nose.

Charlie's eyes widened, and Kit turned in her
saddle to look.

"Oh, no!" she cried. A plume of black smoke rose
above treetops.

"Fire!" Charlie hollered. "I've gotta ring the bell!"
Then he took off.

Kit grabbed the reins, and the newspaper
dropped like a flutter of white wings to the grass,
startling Cloud. The horse jumped sideways, nearly
sending Kit sliding to the ground, but she hung on
to the saddle horn and pulled herself back to center.
Fumbling, she shortened the reins, hoping to gain
control. Cloud pivoted on his back legs, half-rearing,
and bolted toward home.

"Stop! Whoa!" Kit shouted, but Cloud sped up.

Her heart in her throat, Kit clung to the saddle horn as Cloud thundered down the road. What was she supposed to do for a runaway horse? Remembering Benny's instructions on the first day, she pulled the left rein toward her left knee, turning Cloud's head toward her, forcing him to turn in a circle that grew smaller and smaller. Nostrils flaring, Cloud finally slowed to a stop.

Directly across the road in the parking area, a rusty red pickup truck was engulfed in flames. Oily, black smoke swirled in the air. Flames shot up from the truck's engine. Kit gasped. It was the same truck she and Aunt Millie had ridden in with Charlie just a few days earlier.

Big Josh ran from the woods toward Kit, waving his arms. "Go! It might explode!"

Cloud sidestepped and snorted as another truck sped past them toward the fire. Worried that the commotion might make the horse bolt again, Kit turned him and trotted the short distance around the bend. She found Benny where they'd parted, at the grassy entrance by the flagpole. Honey whinnied as Kit rode up.

Benny looked worried. "What's going on?" he asked. "I smell smoke."

"A truck's on fire! It's the same one Charlie rented the other day." Kit swallowed, her throat dry. "Benny, I'm scared for him."

Ba-boom! The horses both startled at the ear-splitting noise.

"We better go," Benny said, turning Honey toward the main road. Kit didn't have to add any pressure to Cloud's sides. He was more than eager to follow.

As the horses broke into a fast-paced trot, Kit drew in several deep breaths, trying to relax as her mind raced with suspicious thoughts.

Big Josh had been the first one on the scene, almost as if he *knew* there would be a fire. He'd even warned her there might be an explosion. Then only moments later, the boom sounded. Big Josh was certainly sad about having to move. And those burns on his hands . . .

Yet none of those suspicions relieved her concerns about Benny. He was unhappy about moving, too. He'd been unfriendly toward the workers as they passed into camp—and instead of joining her to see Charlie, he'd insisted on staying behind. He had the means to start a fire, the same way he had with the torch at the cave. And he would have had plenty of time to start one while she was meeting with Charlie.

The trotting horses startled a ground squirrel on the side of the road, and it scampered away from thudding hooves into the weeds. Kit let her breath out in a whoosh. One second the squirrel was minding its own business, and the next it was nearly trampled to death.

Just like fire and poisonous snakes, thought Kit. In an instant, both could turn deadly.

chapter 9

Ghostly Soldiers

BY THE TIME Kit crawled into bed that night, Aunt Millie was fast asleep. Kit stared at the ceiling, tossing and turning, her pajamas sticking to her skin in the heat. When Aunt Millie drew a deep breath and turned over, Kit whispered: "Aunt Millie? Are you awake?" There was no answer.

Crickets sang outside her window. *Crick-et, crick-et, crick-et, crick-et.*

And then Kit heard something else. *Creak.*

A footstep in the hallway, or someone stepping off the porch outside . . . Was someone sneaking from the house?

Kit tiptoed to the window. Moonlight whitewashed the pasture as sheep grazed.

Creak. The sound rose again from somewhere

below. An old home was filled with creaks and groans, Kit knew. And this home held seven people. Of course she'd hear sounds. But she couldn't help wondering—was Mr. Thatcher heading out for a walk because he couldn't sleep? If so, where exactly did he go when he walked? In his frustration over losing his farm, was he capable of starting fires or planting snakes?

Silent as a mouse in slippers, Kit left the bedroom and made her way down the stairs, one hand on the smooth banister. When she reached the bottom, she glanced through the sewing room's open door at Gran-mammy's bed. Under the mound of blankets, all was quiet. She peered next into the living room, but only the *tick-tick* of the mantle clock broke the silence.

Creak.

Kit caught her breath—she knew that sound: Someone was on the porch, rocking. Kit peered out the living room window to the porch, expecting to see Mr. Thatcher or perhaps Mr. Henry. The small white-haired woman in the rocker surprised her.

It was Gran-mammy!

If Gran-mammy spent all her days in bed, Kit wondered, how did she possibly have the strength to get up and go outside? Or was she not right in her mind? Perhaps she needed help. Kit turned the brass knob and stepped onto the porch.

"Oh! You scared me," Gran-mammy whispered with a jump.

"Sorry. I didn't mean to," Kit said softly. "Is everything all right?"

"Couldn't sleep." Gran-mammy started wheezing and coughing until she doubled over.

Kit hurried inside to the sewing room and returned with a handkerchief. "Here," she said. Then she sat on the top step, her back against the post. "I'll sit with you in case you need help getting back to bed."

Gran-mammy snorted. "Don't worry about me.

It's the soldiers you need to worry about."

"Soldiers?" Kit asked. Did she mean the CCC workers down the road?

"Yes, that's right, soldiers, not so very far from here," Gran-mammy replied impatiently. "I was seventeen when I married Billy, back in sixty-two. Lost him two months later in the Battle of Munfordville. They blew up the bridge to stop 'em from crossing the Green River. But the battle came just the same."

"I'm sorry," Kit whispered, not knowing what else to say. Did Gran-mammy mean *eighteen* sixty-two? Was she talking about a Civil War battle that her first husband, someone named Billy, had fought in—and died in?

Then, with a few stifled gasps, Gran-mammy started to cry. Her breathing was ragged. The night air was damp, and Kit worried that it was too much for Gran-mammy's weak lungs. "They carried so many off that field. And Billy. Oh, I see him now! So perfect! Can you see him?" She stretched both arms in front of her, as if she really did see him.

"So eventually you remarried," Kit said, trying to steer Gran-mammy's mind to more recent years.

"Oh, yes, I married again. For near on forty-two years, raised six ... or was it five? ... children here in this very house. But that's not what wakes me now in the middle of the night. I keep going back to that summer, that terrible autumn ..."

"Gran-mammy," Kit said after a few minutes of silence. She didn't want her to start weeping again. "How about if we both go back to bed and try to get some sleep?"

Kit stepped to the rocker and offered Gran-mammy her hand, but Gran-mammy smacked it away and shouted, her voice raspy. "I don't need an army nurse telling me what to do! Yes, you can carry my husband from the battlefield and tell me he died a hero's death, but part of me died that day, too! So you just keep your hands off me!"

Kit was stunned. Her hand stung. "But I'm just Kit—"

"Oh shush! I am quite capable of managing my affairs, with or without my—"

"Gran-mammy?" Miss Pearl stood in the doorway, arms at the sides of her ghostly pale nightgown.

For a moment, Kit thought Gran-mammy would explode at her daughter-in-law, too. Instead, a wave of comprehension passed across Gran-mammy's face. As if she'd come to the end of a long journey, she sighed and leaned back heavily in the rocking chair.

"You're upset, dear," Miss Pearl said, stepping closer. She stopped at the rocker. "Let's find that bed, shall we?" She took Gran-mammy's elbow and helped her up. This time Gran-mammy cooperated, more like an overly tired child than an outraged adult.

Kit watched as Gran-mammy shuffled along, her head down. How could she have such energy one moment and then seem so frail the next, Kit wondered. Was she faking being sick? Or had her terrible cough come from slipping out some other night? It struck Kit that maybe she had been wrong about the troublemaker's reasons for putting people in danger. If Gran-mammy believed she was surrounded by enemy soldiers in the Civil War, could she have been frightened enough to start that first fire at the Prescott farm? If so, someone else could be responsible for the truck fire at the CCC camp—and the snake in Charlie's trunk.

Over her shoulder, Miss Pearl glanced back at Kit with raised eyebrows, as if to ask what she was doing up with Gran-mammy.

"I heard noises and came downstairs to check," Kit whispered.

"Thank you," Miss Pearl whispered back, as Gran-mammy settled into her bed in the sewing room. "This never used to happen. I'm sorry if she scared you."

"It's okay," Kit replied, and yawned. She climbed

the stairs, her hand still stinging. Gran-mammy might be ninety-three, Kit reflected, but she still had some fire in her belly.

Miss Pearl turned from the griddle on the stove with three pancakes stacked on a spatula. "Who's ready for more?"

JJ piped up. "Yes, ma'am!"

Dorothy Ann pushed back from the table. "May I be excused to look in on Gran-mammy?"

Kit jumped up, anxious to see how Gran-mammy was faring after her strange night. "May I join her?"

"Of course," said Miss Pearl.

Stepping into the sewing room ahead of Kit, Dorothy Ann gasped.

Gran-mammy's head leaned halfway off her pillow. Her eyes were closed. Her mouth hung open.

Kit's heart sank. She was pretty sure Gran-mammy was gone.

Dorothy Ann's wavy hair spread like a dark fan across her back as she leaned over and pressed her ear to Gran-mammy's chest. "Her heart's beating," she whispered to Kit, as she moved Gran-mammy's head and shoulders back to the center of the pillow. "Gran-mammy? Good morning. How are you feeling?"

With a blink of her eyes, Gran-mammy seemed to become aware. "Oh, Pearl . . . It's you."

Dorothy Ann glanced over her shoulder at Kit, a question on her face. Then she turned back. "I'm your granddaughter, Dorothy Ann."

Gran-mammy patted Dorothy Ann's hands with her own, almost as if shaping dough into a round ball. "Of course. Now we better offer some fresh water to those soldiers. They're thirsty, to be sure." She pointed out the window.

"Soldiers?" Dorothy Ann followed her gaze.

Gran-mammy spoke with urgency. "They might be wounded. Cut sheets into bandages. We must do what we can!" Then she started coughing.

Dorothy Ann grabbed Kit by the elbow and stepped out to the foyer. "She must be reliving the Civil War," she whispered, tears springing to her eyes. "She was a young woman back then."

Kit nodded. "She was up last night talking about soldiers."

"Oh dear," Dorothy Ann said, squeezing Kit's hand. "Please, go get my mammy."

Moments later, Miss Pearl hurried into the sewing room ahead of Kit and pressed the back of her hand to Gran-mammy's forehead. "She's awful hot," Miss Pearl said. "Kit, run to the Bransons' and ask Mrs. Branson for her best fever remedy. Go fast."

As Kit raced up the Bransons' long driveway, Bingo leaped off the porch, ran straight for her, and jumped up, paws to her chest, wagging his shaggy gray tail. "You think I came to see you," Kit said, "but I'm on business."

"Hey, Kit," Benny called, stepping outside onto

the front porch. "Ready to ride?"

"Benny," she said, "get your mother, please! Gran-mammy Thatcher is doing poorly."

With a nod of understanding, he darted inside.

When Mrs. Branson stepped out, Kit explained. "Gran-mammy started talking crazy, as if she was remembering things from way back. She's having coughing fits, and now she has a fever. Mrs. Thatcher asked if you have something that might help."

Mrs. Branson drew herself to her full height. "Tickweed tea will ease her cough, and she needs an onion poultice on her chest." She stepped into the house and returned with a cotton satchel tied off with string. "Make tea from these leaves," she said. "For the poultice, boil two onions and mash them up while they're hot. Then put them between two cloths and set it on her chest while its warm. We send our prayers. Now go."

Kit raced back with instructions and helped prepare the poultice with Dorothy Ann. Miss Pearl diligently applied the treatment, but despite her efforts—and the whole house smelling like onions— Gran-mammy began to cough flecks of blood into a handkerchief.

As the sun set that evening, Kit sat at the end of the bed while Dorothy Ann sat near Gran-mammy's head. Suddenly Gran-mammy clutched Dorothy Ann's arm. "Promise me," she whispered, and started wheezing and coughing again.

"Yes, Gran-mammy," said Dorothy Ann. "I promise."

Later, in the living room, Kit asked, "What did you promise her?"

Dorothy Ann's chin rumpled. "I have no idea. She was talking crazy again." Then Dorothy Ann took the stairs two by two to her bedroom and shut the door.

chapter 10

Deep, Dark, and Mysterious

"I'M WORRIED," KIT said, as she and Aunt Millie made their bed the next morning.

"What's on your mind?" asked Aunt Millie.

Kit sighed, not sure where to start. The truck fire proved that Charlie was in real danger. She had serious suspicions about Benny and Big Josh. She even had doubts about JJ and Mr. Henry. And now Gran-mammy was deathly ill.

Kit met Aunt Millie's patient gaze. "What if we can't figure out who's behind the trouble? What if we run out of time and something else happens to Charlie?"

Aunt Millie let out a sigh. "Well, we'll simply have to trust that he can look out for himself. And today is no day for worries. I wanted to surprise you, but now is as good a time as any to tell you that Miss Pearl arranged for a tour of Mammoth Cave this morning with Mr. Branson."

"Oh." Kit knew she should sound more excited, but her worries about Charlie had dampened her enthusiasm about visiting the cave.

"As I recall," Aunt Millie went on, "it's Charlie's day off. I'm sure he'll want to join you."

Kit's heart lifted. "Oh, that's great! Will you come, too?"

"I had intended to join you," Aunt Millie said. "But I really must help Miss Pearl with packing."

After morning chores, JJ agreed to give Kit a ride in the wagon to the CCC camp, where Kit could meet up with Charlie. Then JJ would take them on to the Mammoth Cave entrance. As they pulled out onto the main road, JJ drew a cigarette from his shirt pocket and lit it.

Kit's nose tickled from the smoke. As JJ took a puff of the cigarette, she studied his face intently. "JJ," she said at last. "You told me you didn't smoke. What else aren't you telling me?"

"What do you mean?" JJ shook the hair out of his face and glanced at her sideways, the cigarette dangling in the corner of his lips.

"There was a fire at the CCC camp the other day. I know you're not happy with those guys."

"Come on. That doesn't mean I started a fire."

"Well, somebody did," Kit said.

"You don't say," JJ replied mildly. "You know, for a guest of our hospitality, you sure make some mighty big assumptions."

The weight in Kit's chest turned to a stone in her throat. Her eyes grew hot with tears. "I don't mean to insult you, JJ. I'm sorry. I'm just so worried that something bad might happen to my brother if whoever is doing these things doesn't stop." She wiped her face with the back of her hand.

"Tell you what," JJ said. "I'll keep my eyes open, too. If I see anything out of the ordinary, you'll be the first to know. Sound good?" Then he glanced over with a half smile and a wink.

Kit hesitated. JJ might be bluffing, but what could she say? "Sure. Thanks, JJ."

As JJ's car pulled in to Maple Springs, Kit thought camp seemed a different place on late Sunday morning than it did during the workweek. While JJ waited in the wagon at the entrance, Kit found Charlie in the Education Building, reading in a chair beside a bookcase. Another man sat at a table studying a map.

"Hi, Charlie," Kit whispered, since the other man appeared to be concentrating.

"Kit!" said Charlie, setting aside his book with his bandaged hand. "How great to see you!"

"We're going to tour the cave—at last!" Kit said, her voice rising. "Miss Pearl set up a tour. JJ can take us in the wagon."

Charlie put a finger to his lips. "Shhh. That's

great, but let's keep it down until we're outside."

As they headed through the parking lot, Kit couldn't help looking toward the spot where the burned truck had been. Her stomach twisted when she saw the black halo of soot that still stained the gravel. She wanted to be excited about the cave tour, but now all she could think about was her brother's safety.

"Do you know anything about that truck fire yet?" she asked.

Charlie shrugged. "Nothing yet. The truck was sent to Fort Knox for repairs. The garage there will try to figure out the cause."

"Charlie," Kit said, dropping her voice. "I think I know who started it."

"Who? Did you see someone do it?" Charlie stopped walking and faced Kit.

Kit let out an impatient sigh. "No, I didn't actually see it. But I have two strong suspicions. Either Benny, who was at the flagpole when the fire started, supposedly waiting for me with the horses..."

"Or?"

"Big Josh," Kit said with more certainty. "I stopped my horse near the truck, and who do you guess was the first person to show up?"

Charlie looked shaken. "Big Josh? What makes you say that? Why would *he* want to set that fire?"

"I've been thinking about that. He told me his family has to leave the area. So he would have a good reason to do anything to slow down progress or sabotage the CCC work."

"But if he set the fire, wouldn't he run away instead of going toward it?"

"Well, just like with the copperhead, he shows up as a hero, so no one will suspect him."

Charlie put his hand on Kit's shoulder and squeezed ever so lightly, reminding her of something Dad would do. "Big Josh is my friend, Kit," he said. "There's nothing I wouldn't trust him with. You're barking up the wrong tree."

Kit wished her brother wouldn't be so trusting. If Charlie was right in thinking Big Josh wasn't a risk, that left Benny. But Benny was *her* friend, and she didn't want to suspect him any more than Charlie wanted to suspect Josh.

From the direction of the barracks, a familiar voice rang out. "Look at this!"

Kit and Charlie turned as one toward the sound. To Kit's horror, just outside Charlie's barracks, Big Josh held a snake high in the V of a forked stick. It was another copperhead.

Charlie broke into a run. Kit followed, stopping several yards short of Big Josh.

"Someone put another snake in Charlie's trunk?" Kit asked.

Big Josh chuckled as the two-foot snake curled its tail, trying to get free. He hiked off a distance into the woods, and returned with an empty stick.

"I think I found the source of your snake problem," Big Josh announced. "Somebody left this pile of old boards in a heap under the building." He pointed to the loose boards leaning against the barracks and then to the open space under the building. "I pulled the boards out, thinking we didn't need to invite a snake nest. That's when I spotted the first baby copperhead, maybe eight inches long. Figured where there's one baby, there's more."

"So the one in Charlie's trunk was a she? She laid eggs under there?" Kit asked.

Big Josh gave a nod toward the Education Building. "I found a good book there on snakes. Copperheads incubate eggs inside the female's body, so their babies are born live. One female can give birth to a bunch. Usually between three and nine."

"Nine?" Charlie asked, his eyes wide.

With a nod, Big Josh continued. "Yeah, and though the babies' fangs are tiny, their venom's just as potent as the full-grown ones."

Charlie swallowed. "Sounds like we dodged a bullet! Come on, Kit. We best get going." He saluted

Big Josh. "You're the tops. Thank you!"

Big Josh saluted in return.

Kit wasn't convinced. "That still doesn't explain how a snake got into your trunk," she pointed out as they headed toward JJ's waiting truck.

Charlie just shrugged. "Come on," he said. "We don't want to be late for our cave tour."

Outside the Mammoth Cave Hotel, Mr. Branson was easy to spot with his red bandanna tied around his neck, lantern in hand. He smiled warmly and reached out to shake hands with his customers. "Pleasure to meet you, Kit! Benny and my missus have been talking you up. And you must be Charlie?"

"Yes, sir."

"Have you been on a real tour of the cave yet?" Mr. Branson asked.

"No. Not really," Charlie said.

"Now, before others in our group arrive, I want to

show you where the famous guides are buried." He led them a short way from the hotel to a small clearing and a scattering of headstones.

"Is Floyd Collins here?" Kit asked.

"Kit," Mr. Branson said with a broad smile, "has Benny been telling you stories? Now, here's the real one. Floyd Collins became such a big sensation when he was stuck in the cave that folks capitalized on his fame after his death. To bring in tourists, they even put his body on display at cave entrances, if you can believe that. But he's not buried here."

Mr. Branson leaned against a tombstone and went on. "Many of my ancestors rest here, though. Best guides around in their time. Once you get bitten by the cave bug, it's all you think about."

Within minutes, a dozen more visitors gathered for the tour. "Now, folks," Mr. Branson said, after everyone climbed aboard a small bus with wooden seats, "the Historic Entrance is under construction, so we'll take a short ride over to the New Entrance."

Seated beside Charlie, Kit was nervous and excited all at the same time as the bus shifted into gear. When they stopped at the edge of a leafy woods, Mr. Branson led the way down a sloping path and stopped when he came to a heavy door leading into the side of the hill. "Folks, this is your last chance to turn back. If anyone suffers from vapors, is prone to fainting, has a weak heart, or fear of small spaces, then I strongly suggest you wait in the bus."

Kit tried not to think about Floyd Collins. Maybe she should be like Aunt Millie and stay aboveground, where things were less creepy.

Mr. Branson continued. "Folks, we will descend over two hundred and fifty steps at the start of this journey. If you should find yourself in trouble, there is no fast way to get you out or get help to you. Everyone still in?"

Murmurs of agreement went up from the group. Despite her reservations, Kit nodded.

Mr. Branson unlocked the door with a loud clunk,

and it opened to utter darkness.

The cave emitted a blast of cold air. Pinpricks traveled up Kit's neck and spine as she stepped through the door. It seemed like the entrance to the underworld. Sudden anxiety gripped her. What if she got lost or separated from the group? How would she possibly find her way back out again? Kit wanted to hold Charlie's hand, but the tour was single file on the narrow path.

Within a few steps, daylight vanished.

"Now watch your step," Mr. Branson said. "The stairs can be slippery."

Kit's eyes began to adjust to the light radiating from Mr. Branson's lamp. It illuminated the cave walls and wooden stairs and railings and sent shadows leaping up the cave walls as he moved. The cave suddenly plummeted into a dark chasm to one side of the stairs, then the other. Kit gripped the railing. The stairs led down and down, interrupted by short stretches of rocky path. In spots, the cave walls pressed close, and Kit squeezed through the passages, anxious to stay near the beam of light ahead.

Plink, plink, plink. The cave made a kind of constant music. Mr. Branson's flashlight played along the glistening walls as he explained that the water percolated from aboveground, carving into sandstone as it went. It dripped from cave walls into puddles, rivulets, and streams that flowed deeper and deeper into darkness. *Plink, plink, plink.* Step by step, Kit felt farther and farther from everything familiar.

At the end of the long descent, Mr. Branson led them to a dry, cavernous space complete with wooden benches. "Do you like the benches?" he asked, as Kit and the others found places to sit facing him. "Built by the CCC workers. Built to last, too."

Kit couldn't help feeling proud of Charlie's work, and grateful to Mr. Branson for mentioning it. Though he couldn't be happy about losing his home aboveground, he was generous enough to appreciate what the workers were doing belowground.

"Now this room is called Grand Central Station because of its open space and high ceiling," Mr. Branson went on, explaining that the wide passages were carved by flowing water. Many creatures live here, from crickets and bats to eyeless fish and translucent shrimp in the cave streams. "You see, caverns are always forming. With the passing of time, new caves form dazzling worlds while old caves fill in and eventually disappear."

Kit raised her hand. "The air smells fresh. I thought it might smell bad so far down."

"Yep," Mr. Branson replied. "The cave's constantly moving fresh air in and stale air out. Remember that blast of cold outside the entrance?"

Kit nodded.

"That means that if your light went out, you could find your way back out again. How? Lick your finger, hold it up." Kit did so along with others.

"Which way is the air moving? You follow the current out."

Currents or no, the idea of no light, this far down, made Kit shiver.

The cave *drip, drip, dripped* around them as Mr. Branson led them down another passage. Above, stalactites hung from the ceiling like pillars in a fairy palace.

"These stalactites took many thousands of years to form," Mr. Branson explained. "Water carried minerals to create each one, drop by drop."

From the cave floor, stalagmites rose in pastel colors as cavernous rooms revealed dazzling forms: flows of cream-colored silken drapes, walls of candied popcorn, frozen golden waterfalls, a many-layered skirt, a gaping dragon's mouth.

Kit was filled with awe. She hadn't expected such beauty. It was as if she'd stepped into an art museum, or a church: a sanctuary of quiet, breathtaking beauty. These sculptures were the cave's masterwork—created drop by drop with water over thousands of years, carving, shaping, leaving minerals behind.

And here she stood, deep underground, taking it all in. It made her feel small in the big expanse of time. And yet it gave her a sense of her own significance: Kit realized that every step she took in life, every choice she made, left its mark, too. It was up to her to make sure that her efforts, the marks she made in life, were for the good.

Mr. Branson led them back up to the surface, and Kit stepped into the bright light of day. The leafy canopy overhead and the grass and underbrush at her feet had never looked greener. The sky above with its few wispy clouds had never seemed more blue and infinite. Kit felt relief to be aboveground—yet her sense of joy was more than that. She felt transformed. Being deep inside the cave, seeing its breathtaking natural beauty, had changed her. She saw the world in a new way now—and she realized that she saw herself in a new way, too.

This, Kit realized, was what made Mammoth Cave a national treasure. Kit wanted everyone to be able to see and feel what she had, to experience the mystery of Mammoth Cave. It needed to be protected for future generations.

As the bus started back to the hotel, shadows lengthened. Kit leaned into Charlie's shoulder and gazed out the window. *In the years ahead, when visitors look out like this,* Kit thought, *they won't see a dense patchwork of people, farms, buildings, and billboards—they'll see a quiet green forest.* The work the CCC was doing was protecting the cave and returning the surrounding land to the way it was before settlers changed it. And the tremendous sacrifice by folks like the Thatchers and the Bransons was making it possible for generations to come to be moved and inspired by the cave's beauty and mystery, just as she had been. With sudden conviction, Kit thought to herself, *A national park. It's the right thing to do.*

chapter 11

Where There's Smoke

THAT NIGHT KIT dreamed of the cave. She was lost and trying desperately to find her way out of the tunnels. Bats swooped above and eyeless salamanders hid in the shadows. She woke briefly to a noise . . . like a door creaking in the sewing room below her bedroom . . . Was it Gran-mammy again? Or was it only her imagination? Kit sank back into her dream.

Now smoke was filtering down into the cave, growing so thick it was hard to breathe. If she followed the smoke, she'd find her way out of the cave. And then came a *clang, clang, clang* of a bell. Who would be clanging a bell deep underground? Suddenly the ghost of Floyd Collins was grabbing her, and she screamed.

149

"Kit!" Floyd—or *someone*—shook her shoulders. "Wake up! There's a fire!"

The clanging continued from somewhere outside.

Kit blinked awake and tasted smoke. "Aunt Millie? What's going on?"

"I don't know, but there's a fire," Aunt Millie said. "Get your shoes on. Hurry!"

Kit tried to clear her mind and separate her dream from reality. "Is the house on fire?"

"I'm not sure," said Aunt Millie, pulling her up. "Let's go!"

Kit flew down the staircase after Aunt Millie, her nightgown billowing. They nearly tumbled into Miss Pearl and Mr. Thatcher in the kitchen. Outside, Dorothy Ann was a silhouette against a bright fire that was creeping across a field on the Thatcher farm. With two hands, she clanged a steel bar around the inside of a triangular gong. *Bong, bong, bong.* Kit recognized the sound she had heard in her dream.

She glanced around. "Where's JJ?"

"He just left to tell the Bransons," Miss Pearl replied.

The door of the handyman's cottage opened and Mr. Henry raced out, pulling suspenders up over his shoulders. "What should we do?" he asked, joining them.

Mr. Thatcher pointed toward the barn. "We need to make a human chain for water buckets. That wind's shifted. It's pushing that fire straight for us!"

Fire lit up the sky. Plumes of black smoke chugged upward, as if a giant dragon—all smoke and flames— were making its way toward the Thatchers' farm.

Dorothy Ann looked toward the oncoming fire, face aglow as she pressed her hands to her lips.

Kit's every nerve was on high alert.

"Kit," Miss Pearl said, facing her. "We need you to stay with Gran-mammy while we put out the fire. If she wakes up, she might get scared and try to get out of bed. We'll keep the house safe."

"But I want to help fight the fire," Kit said. The

last place she wanted to be was inside the clapboard farmhouse as the fire raged.

"Kit," Aunt Millie said, "this is no time to argue. Do as Miss Pearl says."

So Kit watched from the kitchen window as Aunt Millie, Miss Pearl, Mr. Thatcher, and Dorothy Ann scurried across the farmyard, back and forth, lugging buckets and tossing water against the walls of the barn and chicken coop. If the fire reached the farm, she knew, it would hit those buildings first.

The wind drove smoke through the house. Kit closed the kitchen window, trying to keep it out. Then she ran around the house closing all the windows. If the fire came close, it would leap through the screens and set everything on fire—curtains, bedspreads, furniture . . . even the heirloom spinning wheel! Then she checked on Gran-mammy.

From her bed in the sewing room, Gran-mammy's thin, knobby hands wove through the air, as if she were spinning wool into thread. And yet her eyes were closed. She wasn't coughing, but each breath seemed to take great effort. She murmured something, but Kit couldn't make sense of it. Kit sat in the chair at the bedside, wondering if she should sneak back to the kitchen. Suddenly, Gran-mammy reached out and grabbed Kit's arm. "Promise!" she croaked.

That word again—the same one she'd said to Dorothy Ann.

"Promise what?" Kit asked her.

Gran-mammy mumbled, eyes closed.

"It's okay, Gran-mammy Thatcher," Kit said softly. "You go back to sleep."

But the truth was, Kit couldn't tell if Gran-mammy was asleep or awake. She seemed to be in a faraway place.

When the roar of truck engines and the clamor of voices came from outside, Kit carefully peeled Gran-mammy's fingers from her arm. She had to see what was happening. She raced to the kitchen and stepped outside. The wind howled and carried sparks. In only a few minutes' time, the fire had crossed the field and leaped closer to the outbuildings.

"Kit! Stay there!" It was Charlie's voice. Kit searched for him among a group of CCC workers racing from a truck near the driveway. Many carried shovels and ran toward the approaching fire. Others were already at the pump, filling bucket after bucket and hurrying with them toward the barn. After a moment, Kit spotted Charlie, his shovel raised skyward, trying to get her attention.

She waved back, wishing she could be with him, helping.

How had the fire begun? Kit wondered. But in her heart, she knew. There hadn't been any lightning in the sky or any other natural way for a fire to start, so that meant someone must have started it on purpose.

Kit thought of JJ and Mr. Henry. She didn't trust either of them. But why start a fire that would burn down your own farm?

Then she remembered what Mr. Thatcher had

said. *The wind had shifted.* When Kit had gone to bed, the breeze blew in her screen window out of the west, cooling her above her covers. Now it had changed, coming straight out of the east. Someone like JJ or Mr. Henry might have started a fire, thinking it would burn toward the Green River. Of course the CCC would have to work at containing any fires. It would set them back a few days in their other work. But then the wind had shifted, sending the fire in the opposite direction, right toward the Thatchers' and Bransons' barns and homes.

"Keep the water coming!" Mr. Thatcher shouted.

Kit's throat burned with smoke. She wanted to be part of the bucket brigade! She didn't want to be stuck in the house. Not at a time like this!

Another truck pulled up, and the Branson family spilled out. Benny had a bucket, ready to help. He waved and she lifted her hand in return, feeling the hot glow of fire on her face. With a sigh, she headed back inside to check on Gran-mammy.

"Kit!" She turned as Dorothy Ann rushed across the grass to the kitchen door. Her face was damp with sweat, and her lilac-colored blouse above her trousers was splotchy with ash and mud. "How's Gran-mammy?" Dorothy Ann asked between panting breaths.

"She's in bed, but she seems somewhere else," Kit told her.

Dorothy Ann glanced over her shoulder. Beyond, workers scurried like ants. "Now that they're here, I can take over for you."

On the wind, the sharp, piney scent of turpentine slipped past. "Smell that?" Kit asked. "Turpentine. I bet someone used it to start the fire."

Dorothy Ann pressed her hand to her throat. "All I smell is smoke. Now go; they could use your help."

As Kit bolted toward the barn and the human chain of buckets, she stayed alert for anyone carrying the scent of turpentine on their trousers, boots, or gloves.

When she found Aunt Millie, she tapped her back. Above the sound of blowing wind, chugging fire, and men yelling orders, Kit shouted, "Dorothy Ann wants to stay with Gran-mammy. I'm here to help!"

Aunt Millie nodded and motioned for Kit to work beside her. Kit grabbed one bucket of water, then another, and another, and handed them to Aunt Millie, who passed them down the line. The buckets were heavy, and Kit's shoulders pinched, but she couldn't stop. If the fire reached the barn, filled with this season's hay, it would go up like a torch.

Kit wished she could get a breath of pure air, but smoke entered her mouth with every breath.

"Don't slosh the water!" someone shouted. "Make sure it reaches the barn!"

The roar of the fire grew louder and closer, and the sky was filled with sparks, as if it were raining red stars. At the barn, workers threw water at glowering flames. In the distance, others bent over earth with shovels. Kit knew they were digging ditches to expose bare earth, hoping the fire would stop where it had nothing left to consume.

"Kit!" Aunt Millie ruffled the top of Kit's head. "A spark!"

The putrid smell of burned hair filled Kit's nose. She reached up and patted her head, glad to find she still had hair there.

A fire truck arrived with a giant cistern and long hose. Men quickly unwound the hose and aimed it at the barn, soaking its side. More workers arrived from other camps to help fight the fire.

With all the noise and commotion, Kit wondered whether Gran-mammy had awakened. If she looked out the window, thought Kit, she would surely think she was back in the Civil War, with smoke and shouting and young men scrambling everywhere.

And then a hush fell all around. Something had changed.

"The wind stopped!" Kit shouted. A round of cheers went up from the shadowy landscape.

Aunt Millie wiped her forehead. "Now we have a chance of containing the fire."

But before Kit could manage a breath of relief, the wind picked up again. It gusted the fire to life, sending it arcing in a different direction. Kit spotted Benny and Mr. Branson racing off. Several workers hopped in trucks and ran on foot toward the Branson farm.

Kit scanned the pasture for the sheep and spotted them pressed against the far edge of the fence, little puffs of white in the distance. The fire climbed higher and belched up another cloud of black smoke. The pasture lay directly in its path. If the fire advanced, the sheep wouldn't be able to escape it. She raced inside to tell Dorothy Ann.

"The fire's headed toward the sheep!" Kit cried. "They'll be trapped!"

"Oh no!" Dorothy Ann flew out of the sewing room, slamming the kitchen door in her wake.

Kit prayed that Dorothy Ann would reach the

sheep before the fire did. Whoever had started this terrible fire, Kit hoped he would be found out soon—and brought to justice.

chapter 12
A Distressing Discovery

KIT WATCHED FROM the kitchen window as the fire roared in the distance. Wind fanned the flames, sending sparks flying toward the Bransons' farm.

Deep, hacking coughs came from the sewing room. "Water, please," came Gran-mammy's thin voice. When Kit stepped in, Gran-mammy was resting against her pile of pillows, her skin gray and her eyes closed and sunken.

"I'll bring you some," Kit said as calmly as possible. Gran-mammy seemed to have no sense that a wildfire was under way, and Kit saw no good reason to upset her.

When Kit returned from the kitchen, Gran-mammy drank half the water, then tried to put the glass back on her bedside table. But her hand trembled, and she let go too soon. The glass tumbled and shattered against the metal bed frame on its way to the floor.

"Oh, I'm sorry," Gran-mammy said heavily. "I'll clean it up."

"You just rest there, Gran-mammy," Kit replied. "I'll take care of it."

Kit found a rag, a broom, and dustpan. When she returned, Gran-mammy was fast asleep. Kit swept the broken shards into the dustpan. She lifted the edge of the bedspread and probed with her broom for more shards under Gran-mammy's bed.

The broom hit something tinny. The faint scent of turpentine reached Kit's nose.

On her hands and knees, Kit peered under the bed and spotted a cloth sack. Curious, she pulled it toward her, loosened its drawstring, and looked inside.

"Oh no," Kit mouthed silently. There were strips

of damp cotton rags—she recognized their sharp, piney smell in an instant. An empty turpentine can. And a box of matches.

But who would hide this under Gran-mammy's bed? And why? Certainly it was the last place anyone would look for it. Kit closed up the sack, pushed it back under the bed, and quietly stood, expecting to meet Gran-mammy's accusing eyes. But she was sleeping, her chest rising and falling slowly in deep breaths.

Or pretending to sleep.

Did Gran-mammy know who had set the fire? In her mind, Kit reviewed the small gap of time between when she'd first learned of the fire and found Dorothy Ann sounding the alarm. The one person Kit hadn't seen outside the farmhouse, the one person who could have slipped into Gran-mammy's room to hide evidence before going off to alert the Bransons of the fire—the very fire he'd probably started—was JJ. Had he trusted Gran-mammy with his secret?

Kit tiptoed out slowly, anxious to tell Aunt Millie and Miss Pearl about her discovery. But the house was quiet. Everyone was gone, fighting the fire at the Bransons' farm.

Kit had no choice but to wait.

The rooster crowed, startling Kit. She opened her eyes, trying to piece together where she was and why. She remembered trying to keep her eyes open through the long night, but eventually she'd curled up under a quilt on the braided rug beside Gran-mammy's bed.

She sat up and pushed her hair out of her eyes.

Last night's fire seemed like a nightmare, but the air tasted bitter, acrid with smoke. It was no dream. As her eyes adjusted, she breathed a sigh of relief. The farmhouse had survived. But what about the sheep? What about the Bransons?

Kit pushed aside the quilt, stood up, and glanced

at Gran-mammy, remembering her discovery under the bed. She had half a mind to wake Gran-mammy up and confront her.

But Gran-mammy seemed awfully still.

Something didn't seem right.

Kit leaned down.

Listening for the sound of breathing, Kit peered more closely at Gran-mammy's face. "Gran-mammy?" The old woman's eyes were closed, her face slack. Kit watched for the faint rise and fall of Gran-mammy's chest.

Nothing.

Kit touched her hand. The skin was cool.

Too cool.

Gran-mammy was gone.

Kit swallowed hard, fighting the urge to cry. Gran-mammy had been alive through most of that crazy, smoke-filled night. And now she was . . . still as stone. Kit couldn't bring herself to even think the word. She scrambled out of the room, raced upstairs, ready to pound on bedroom doors. But all the doors were wide open. No one, not even Aunt Millie, was there.

Oh, to be alone in the house with Gran-mammy! It was too strange.

Kit ran back down the staircase and tiptoed back into the sewing room. Maybe she'd been wrong. Maybe Gran-mammy was only sleeping . . .

She stood in the door frame, gazing at the too-still figure on the bed. No. Gran-mammy was definitely gone.

Kit threw on her shoes by the kitchen door and bolted outside. The sun was just rising. Where woods once rose at the eastern edge of the pasture, leafless charred trees now stood. The ground was scorched to bare earth not far from the barn. Kit spotted the sheep, now penned in a different pasture. Dorothy Ann must have managed to get them to safety in time. The only sound of life came from chickens wanting out of their coop.

Kit hurried over, raised the small coop door, and let the chickens out. The rooster hopped out first, ruffled his feathers, then strutted across the yard. One after one, hens hopped out, clucking and humming, heads bobbing to the ground. At the end of the line, First Lady hopped out. Seven brown peeping chicks the size of golf balls darted around her legs.

"Oh!" Kit shook her head. The chicks must have hatched overnight. Her eyes pricked with tears. How could death and new life fill the same moment?

The rising sun revealed a night's worth of labor against the fire. The earth was muddy around the barn, and stray buckets waited to be reclaimed. A shovel here. A pitchfork there. Deep ruts from the fire truck remained in the grass.

"Everyone must be at the Bransons'," she said aloud. Maybe it wasn't right to leave a body, but she couldn't bear to stay here, alone, waiting. And she had to let the Thatchers know. She started down the driveway, walking, then running, her nightgown wrapping around her knees and threatening to trip her.

When she turned into the Bransons' driveway, CCC trucks filled with workers passed, returning to camp. Kit lifted her hand. They returned her tired wave. She looked for Charlie but didn't see him.

At the Bransons' farmhouse porch, a group was gathered—Bransons, Thatchers, and folks Kit didn't know. Beyond the house, smoke rose from the barn, or what was left of it, a towering pile of water-doused boards.

Enclosed in a nearby pasture, pigs were clustered at the fence line, waiting to be fed.

Bingo raced out to meet her, wagging his tail as if it were any ordinary day. But this was no ordinary day. She had news to deliver—the biggest news of her life. But how could she say it? What words could she use?

"Kit!" Aunt Millie cried. "What a night we've had!"

"Is Charlie okay?" Kit asked as she drew near. "Did anybody get hurt?"

Then Charlie stepped down from the porch. His face was smudged with ash, his trousers were mud-splattered, and he'd never looked better to Kit.

She gave him a fierce hug. "I was worried about you!"

"I'm fine, Kit," Charlie said, hugging her back.

Kit looked around. "Where's Benny?"

Mrs. Branson answered. "He's inside sleeping. You'll be glad to know he rescued those kittens last night, with not a moment to lose."

"Oh, thank goodness," Kit said with relief.

The sun rose higher, revealing the fatigue on everyone's faces as the crowd broke apart and people moved off to their trucks and cars.

"Come on, Pearl," Mr. Thatcher said. "Better head back so someone's around for Gran-mammy." He waved to JJ, Dorothy Ann, Aunt Millie, and Kit to join him. "We've also got chores to do."

Kit tried to find the words, but nothing seemed right. She reached for Aunt Millie's hand and held fast. Maybe it would be best if the Thatchers made their own discovery when they returned home. Kit didn't want to be the one to tell them.

"Aunt Millie, can we walk back?"

"Sure, if you'd like."

As they walked, the last remaining CCC truck passed them. Charlie waved from the truck bed. It was all Kit could do to raise her arm and wave back.

chapter 13

A Promise

ON THE SHORT walk back to the Thatchers' farm, Kit slowed her pace. She wanted to give the Thatchers time to make their sad discovery while she told Aunt Millie about Gran-mammy.

Aunt Millie put her arm around Kit's shoulder. "Oh Kit! I'm so sorry you had to face death alone. If you live a long life, it won't be your last time, but it's always hard when it comes."

"I feel so bad that her family wasn't with her when she died," Kit said.

Aunt Millie nodded. "They'll wish so, too, but with the fire, it's just lucky their house didn't go up in flames. Gran-mammy didn't die alone, Kit. You were there. That will bring the family comfort."

As they reached the Thatchers' front door, fiddle

music drifted toward them. Not fast, leg-stomping music, but a sweet and slow melody. Kit followed Aunt Millie to the sewing room, where the Thatcher family was crowded together, singing beside Granmammy's bed.

Aunt Millie joined in on the refrain:

> *Yes, we'll gather at the river,*
> *The beautiful, the beautiful river;*
> *Gather with the saints at the river*
> *That flows by the throne of God.*

Kit looked around at the family. Mr. Thatcher was kneeling beside the bed, his head bowed. Miss Pearl's and Dorothy Ann's eyes overflowed. With the fiddle tucked under his chin and his eyes closed, JJ played another tune.

Kit swallowed back tears. Now they knew Granmammy was gone.

But how could she tell them about the sack under

the bed? As unlikely as it seemed, the evidence pointed to both JJ and Gran-mammy. Was it better to leave the family with their good memories? Or to tell the truth?

A knock sounded on the front door, startling Kit. "I'll get it," she said, and closed the sewing room door behind her.

"Charlie!" she said, her tone hushed as she opened the front door wide to let him in. Beside him stood a park ranger with graying sideburns.

"Kit, this is Officer O'Dell," Charlie said.

The park ranger dipped his head. "Hello, Kit. Charlie's talked about you."

Charlie continued. "Officer O'Dell thought it would be helpful if I came along to check in with the Thatchers after the fire. He needs to begin investigating the cause as quickly as possible. Will you get Mr. and Mrs. Thatcher, please?"

Kit hesitated. "Things are difficult here right now," she told them, adding, "Gran-mammy Thatcher passed away early this morning."

"I'm sorry to hear that," Officer O'Dell said. "Bad news never comes at a good time, does it."

"Um, no, sir. Could you wait here, please?" Kit motioned to the living room sofa. Then she crossed the room and eased open the sewing room door with Officer O'Dell's words ringing in her ears: *Bad news never comes at a good time.*

Kit cleared her throat. "I'm sorry to interrupt. My brother is here with a park ranger, Officer O'Dell. They need to talk with Mr. and Mrs. Thatcher about the fire. But first, I have something to say." She closed the door behind her. "Something difficult."

Aunt Millie put her hand on Miss Pearl's shoulder.

"I need to show you what I found under Granmammy's bed," Kit went on. She dropped to her knees, reached under the bed for the sack, and held it up. "I think the things in here were used to start the fire. And I think I know who did it."

JJ crossed his arms and wagged his head. "You

just won't let it go that somebody here is guilty, will you?"

"No," Kit said, glaring back at him. She loosened the sack's drawstring and held it open. "Matches, strips of rags, and here"—she pulled out the can—"an empty can of turpentine. Who would put *that* in a sack under a bed, unless they were trying to hide evidence? It's the one thing that wouldn't burn if it was left behind at the fire."

JJ took the sack from Kit's hands, examining it.

Kit tried to read his face. Was he trying to act innocent, as if he'd never seen the sack before?

"Kit!" Miss Pearl said with disbelief. "There's no way Gran-mammy could have made it more than a few feet in her condition. You can't possibly think she was involved."

"That's ridiculous," Mr. Thatcher added. He stood at the foot of the bed, arms crossed. "Gran-mammy could barely lift her head off the pillow."

"I'm not saying Gran-mammy—" Kit began.

Dorothy Ann cut in, her voice just above a whisper, her dark eyes pleading. "Y'all, Gran-mammy knew her time was near. She desperately wanted to die at home. She didn't want anyone to get hurt. She just wanted to slow down time. If the camp workers were delayed by putting out a fire by a few days, then that gave her a few more days. Don't you see?" Tears coursed down her ash-smudged cheeks.

"What?" Kit was baffled by Dorothy Ann's words. Was *she* saying Gran-mammy had something to do with this? It was true that the old woman had shown some spirit and little bursts of strength toward the end, but surely it was JJ who'd started the fire and hidden the evidence.

A long moment of silence passed as Kit and the rest of the Thatchers looked at Dorothy Ann in disbelief.

"Oh, I can't lie. I can't have you thinking she did it!" Dorothy Ann sobbed. "I loved Gran-mammy so much!" Her sorrow nearly broke Kit's heart.

Dorothy Ann held her palms up, as if pleading for mercy from everyone in the room. "Truth be told, Gran-mammy begged me! She was desperate for me to find a way for her to stay here, to die in the place where she was born. The fire at the Prescotts' place got me to thinking. I didn't want to cause trouble, but I had to find a way for her to die at home in peace. She made me *promise*!"

Kit blinked at the word. When she'd asked Dorothy Ann about the "promise," Dorothy Ann had stood at the foot of the staircase and said she had no idea what Gran-mammy was talking about. And last night, when Kit met Dorothy Ann outside and caught the scent of turpentine, Dorothy Ann had again denied any knowledge, declaring all she could smell was smoke. With a sinking heart, Kit realized that the smell had come from Dorothy Ann herself.

Dorothy Ann continued, her voice watery with tears. "I swear, I . . . I didn't want anyone to get hurt. That's why I rang the bell."

It was suddenly clear to Kit why the sack had ended up under Gran-mammy's bed. "You didn't want anyone to find evidence, the way they had at the first fire. So last night you set the fire, came back here, and hid everything," Kit said.

"Yes!" Dorothy Ann said. "I thought no one would notice it there, at least until I could take it somewhere else. And I truly thought the fire would burn toward the river, but then the wind shifted toward us! I panicked. It was out of control. Then it switched again, toward the Bransons'. I was terrified of what might happen!" She bowed her head, sobbing.

Miss Pearl reached for her daughter's shoulders and pulled her close. "Oh, if you'd only told us. Gran-mammy had no right to put you in such a position, to make you promise such a thing. It wasn't right for her to ask it of you. And it wasn't right for you to do what you did, either."

"I know!" Dorothy Ann moaned. "I'm so sorry."

Three knocks came on the sewing room door.

Kit opened it.

In the door frame stood Officer O'Dell. He cleared his throat, announcing his presence. "Excuse me," he said. "I understand the eldest Thatcher passed last night." He looked at the bed and the sheet drawn over Gran-mammy's face. "I'm mighty sorry for your loss." He removed his hat and held it to his chest.

"Did you hear everything?" Dorothy Ann asked, her braid half undone and face and eyes red from crying. "Are you going to arrest me?"

For several moments, no one said a word.

"Might we all talk in the living room?" Officer O'Dell said finally.

As if carrying great stones, every member of the Thatcher family slowly followed Officer O'Dell to the parlor. Dorothy Ann sat down at her spinning wheel, hands in her lap and head bowed. Kit sat close by on the stool.

"I came to discuss last night's fire, as well as the

letter you received a few weeks ago," said the officer. "The fire will certainly set us back at least a day or two. First, the boys are going to need to get some rest. In a few hours, I'll put them back out on the burn sites with axes and shovels until everything is out cold. We can't risk any smoldering embers. There's too much fuel out there. Last night made that clear enough. We need to thin some of the undergrowth or we could end up with a fire we can't stop."

Kit exchanged glances with Charlie. The park ranger acted as if he hadn't heard a bit of the conversation in the sewing room, but he'd have to be deaf not to have heard Dorothy Ann's confession. Charlie's face showed no reaction, though, so Kit decided to wear the same calm expression too.

Officer O'Dell continued, his voice solemn. "Today is a hard day." He looked around the room from person to person. "I had planned to come here to remind you that tomorrow is your day to vacate your property. But, under the circumstances, I see no reason why we can't extend that a bit. I know it's not your wish to leave." He turned to Mr. Thatcher and Miss Pearl. "We recognize that you are making a big sacrifice for this nation by leaving your family farm. So before we begin removing a single board, I'll send over a few young men to help you with burial needs."

"But where can we bury her?" Mr. Thatcher blurted, his voice cracking. "Even our church and cemetery are in the park boundaries now."

Officer O'Dell nodded. "I'm pleased to tell you that the park has agreed to keep the churches within its borders open to their members. That means you and your kin can continue to attend Good Springs Church and bury your loved ones there as you have for generations."

"Praise God," Miss Pearl said.

"Mr. and Mrs. Thatcher," Charlie asked softly, "do you know what you'll do next? Where you'll go?"

Mr. Thatcher took his wife's hand. "Late yesterday I found a spot a few miles outside the park. Still in

Hart County. What with the fire—and now Gran-mammy—I haven't had a chance to share the news. The farm has two hundred acres of hay fields and fenced pasture. The owners are older folks who are moving to town, and they've agreed to rent it to us for a year. If it works out, we can buy it."

Kit glanced over at Dorothy Ann. Her dark locks nearly covered her face. Teardrops struck the floor-boards at her bare feet.

A swirl of emotions swept through Kit like a torrent of water, carving and reshaping everything it touched. Perhaps Dorothy Ann hadn't intended for anyone to get hurt, yet starting the fire had put Charlie and many other people at risk. Someone could have *died.*

Livestock, including the pigs and sheep, could have died. Even the kittens in the Bransons' barn could have died.

Gran-mammy should have died peacefully at home surrounded by family. Yet the park's clock had ticked off the hours and minutes until their eviction. None of that seemed fair. Without a doubt, Kit knew that Dorothy Ann loved Gran-mammy and wanted to honor her dying wish: *to die in the home where she was born.*

Yet, as Miss Pearl had said, it had been unfair of Gran-mammy to put that burden on her granddaughter. If she'd been in Dorothy Ann's predicament, Kit asked herself, what would she have done?

Officer O'Dell's voice interrupted Kit's thoughts. "About last night's fire," he said. "The Bransons' barn burned down. Due to quick action by the neighbors and the CCC, no one was hurt, and no livestock were lost. But let me be clear, the intentional starting of fires—*arson*—is a most serious crime indeed."

Dorothy Ann nodded, and then spoke without lifting her head. "The other fire, the one at the Prescott place, wasn't my doing," she said, her voice scarcely a whisper. "You've got to believe me."

Charlie's response came swiftly. "We know. It was

in our camp newspaper yesterday. A property owner from the other side of the park admitted to setting that fire in retaliation for losing his own house."

Officer O'Dell nodded. "That's right. The fellow's conscience got to bothering him about it. He said he had to confess if he could ever hope for a good night's sleep again." Then he paused.

Kit held her breath.

"Given the unusual circumstances we find our-selves in today," Officer O'Dell said slowly, and paused again. He looked at Dorothy Ann, who must have sensed his eyes on her.

She lifted her face, her eyelids swollen. Her lips trembled as she spoke. "Gran-mammy helped bring me up. She taught me everything I know about raising sheep, spinning, knitting," she said in a quavering voice. "I guess I would have given my life for her if I could have."

Officer O'Dell looked at Dorothy Ann for what seemed an eternity, as if he was struggling mightily

to find a solution. First he moved his hat from his
chest back to his head. He pushed his shoulders back,
as if what he was going to say was going to take more
strength than he possessed.

"Winter's coming before long," he said, his words
surprising Kit. "Over at Maple Springs, there are lots
of young men who could use a pair of good wool
socks. You know how to knit socks?"

Dorothy Ann nodded.

"And are you fast?"

Again she nodded.

"Then how about you knit up a storm between
now and spring? Each week you deliver to the camp
as many pairs as you can make. Over the winter
months ahead, every worker at the camp will look
forward to a new pair of socks. That's a whole lot of
socks. My mother knits, so I know you'll be doing
nothing else between now and spring. It would be a
mighty fine act of charity. Could you agree to that,
young lady?"

His words brought a fresh round of tears from Dorothy Ann, but she wiped her face with the back of her hands, snuffled, and then whispered, "Yes. I want to make things right. I'll make warm, sturdy socks out of the finest wool. I promise."

chapter 14

Home

WHILE OFFICER O'DELL finished talking with Dorothy Ann and her parents, Kit waited outside with Charlie on the front porch. He hadn't had a chance to clean up or change his clothes since fighting the fire.

"Your boots are still soaking wet," she said, noticing the darkened leather.

He nodded. "They get wet a lot, especially working down in the cave. But they always dry out fast in the sun."

Out of nowhere, an image flashed through Kit's head. It was of Charlie stumbling over someone's belongings on that very first day they visited his barracks. "Do you leave your boots to dry on your porch step?" she asked, her mind jumping ahead.

"Sure. How did you know?"

"There was stuff drying on the steps the day you found the snake. Charlie, I bet that's how you got a snake in your trunk! Dorothy Ann said they like to find warm, cozy places to sleep. What better place than a warm boot left out in the sun?"

A smile crept across Charlie's face. "Of course! I'd left my boots out to dry just the day before. I bet a copperhead crawled inside and hitched a ride to my trunk when I put them away for the night." He looked at his boots. "Just to be safe, I'm finding a nice patch of sunshine *inside* the barracks where these can dry."

Kit leaned against the wooden porch post. "Well, that explains the snake. And now we know who started the fires, but that still leaves the truck fire."

"Oh, in all the confusion, I completely forgot to tell you," Charlie said. "The report came back from Fort Knox yesterday morning. Turns out it was just a faulty wire in the truck engine."

At this information, Kit felt the last knot inside

her loosen. "Oh, what a relief," she exclaimed.

"Yeah, but not for my friend Joe. He was making a tidy sum renting it out. Now his plans to get rich are on hold until it's fixed."

Kit crossed her arms. "Well, at least now I can quit worrying about you while you're here at the park."

"Oh, don't do that," said Charlie, the corners of his eyes gathering into a grin.

"Why not?" Kit tilted her head, bracing herself for some of Charlie's teasing.

"Because, sometimes I'm going to be working deep in the caves. Peculiar things happen down there." He winked. "You never know, Floyd Collins might tap me on the shoulder someday."

Kit rolled her eyes. "Well, if he does, just say hello for me, okay?"

Before leaving the next morning, Kit found JJ in the barn, milking a cow. "I wanted to say good-bye,"

Kit said, "and that I'm sorry for thinking it was you."

With a toss of his head, JJ glanced up at her. "It's been a pretty crazy time around here. But I've got a few songs in my head because of it all."

"You do?" Kit smiled. She knew she shouldn't feel surprised. Music seemed to run through his blood.

"Maybe you'll hear one of them on the radio one of these days. You never know."

Next, Kit went to say good-bye to Dorothy Ann. She found her cleaning Dixie's hooves, and suddenly Kit didn't know what to say. Dorothy Ann seemed at a loss for words, too. She glanced up at Kit. Then she set down the horse's foot, straightened up tall, and the girls hugged each other hard.

"So long," Kit said. "Thank you for having me."

"So long," Dorothy Ann replied. "I'm forever grateful you were here with Gran-mammy when she passed. Thank you, Kit."

Soon Kit and Aunt Millie were seated beside Mr. Thatcher in the wagon. Miss Pearl stood beside them, her hand grasping Aunt Millie's. "Next time you two come this way, you'll stay with us again. Promise?"

"Promise," Aunt Millie and Kit said at once.

"Wait, y'all!" Benny came running down the drive carrying a small wooden crate. "I'm riding along to see them off!"

"Finally," Mr. Thatcher said, as if he'd been expecting Benny.

Benny climbed in the wagon beside their luggage. When they drove past the Maple Springs turnoff, Kit wanted one more good-bye with Charlie, but it was a Tuesday, so he was off working with his crew. She silently wished him an *unpeculiar* time ahead at camp.

When Dixie stepped off the ferry, pulling the wagon onto the opposite shore of the Green River, a familiar figure walked ahead alongside the road, his rucksack stuffed to overflowing.

"That's Mr. Henry," Kit said.

"Sure enough," Mr. Thatcher agreed, easing back on the reins.

"Mr. Henry!" Kit said, as they slowed. "You left this morning before we had a chance to say good-bye. Where will you go next?"

"Next place that'll have me," he said with a smile that showed his crooked teeth. "And turns out, the park here wants someone to demonstrate basket-making, to keep the skill alive and show visitors. I'm thinking I might try my hand at that. They'll even provide me a small cabin and wages."

"Good for you, Mr. Henry," Aunt Millie said.

He tipped his fedora and gave a nod of good-bye as they continued on.

When they arrived at the Mammoth Cave Hotel, their train waited, rumbling, as if impatient to get going. Aunt Millie and Kit shook hands with Mr. Thatcher, thanking him for his hospitality. "And our sympathy, again, on the loss of your mother," Aunt Millie said, speaking for Kit as well.

"There is a time to be born and a time to die," Mr. Thatcher said. "Ain't that the truth for all of us?"

Benny kept his distance until Kit and Aunt Millie were about to board the train.

"Benny," Kit said. "I apologize for thinking you started any fires or put a snake in the barracks. You made my trip extra special by taking me to see your special cave, and swimming, and teaching me to handle a horse. I had a swell time. Thank you! If you're ever in Cincinnati, you'll have to come visit me."

He nodded, as if he would like to, but that the miles between them might be too great. "When you come back someday, I'll show you more of the cave. By then I bet I'll have discovered new passages!"

"I'd like that," Kit said.

"Now promise," Benny said, pushing the wooden crate into Kit's hands. A soft mewing sound rose from inside. Kit's eyes widened.

"You can't open the lid until you're gone from the station. Promise?"

"I promise!" Kit told him, excitement bubbling up as Benny spun away and dashed in the direction of the Historic Entrance to Mammoth Cave. Kit realized she hadn't asked him what their plans were for when they packed up their belongings and left their farm. She wished the Bransons could stay. She wished they had another place to call home. The clock was ticking for them, too.

"Come on, Kit," Aunt Millie said from the train step. "Let's get aboard."

Kit held the crate fast to her chest, climbed the steps, and settled into a seat.

"Well, what do you have there?" Aunt Millie asked with a playful grin.

"Aunt Millie!" Kit exclaimed. "Why, you know, don't you?"

As the train blew its whistle and lurched forward, Kit waved at Mr. Thatcher, who waved his hat back at them in return. When the hotel had disappeared from view, Kit couldn't wait a second longer. She was dying to look inside the wooden crate, even though she was pretty sure she knew what she'd find. She lifted the top—and two sets of bright eyes looked back.

"Oh! Aunt Millie! I knew it. But I didn't expect two!" She lifted out the calico kitten and handed him to Aunt Millie. "This is Shakespeare. He's yours, if you want him."

"Good choice for a name!" Aunt Millie exclaimed. She held the kitten up and gazed at its tiny face. "Aren't you a sight for sore eyes?"

Kit picked up the charcoal gray kitten and held it to her chest. "This one is Smoky." Then the reality of taking two kittens home to their bustling house hit her. "But what will Mother and Dad say? What if they won't—"

"Just put those worries to rest," Aunt Millie said, as she lifted Shakespeare to her neck. "Benny planned this with me since the day you first named these kittens. I had Charlie use the CCC phone to call your parents to make sure it would be okay with them."

Kit felt a smile grow. So much had happened to her on this trip—hard things, but good things, too. Her feelings about it all still felt a little tangled, the good with the bad, but she knew one thing for sure: She would never forget the things that she had seen and learned at Mammoth Cave.

As the train picked up speed and hurtled forward, Kit sat back in her seat with a contented sigh. Right now it was enough to enjoy the small, simple things—like the rhythmic rumble of the train and the kitten in her lap. She stroked his soft-as-silk charcoal fur. Smoky looked up at her with sky blue eyes. His purring flowed like a river straight into Kit's heart, carving out a home.

Inside Kit's World

Chances are that you, like Kit, have visited one of America's amazing national parks—or you will at some time in your life. Today, the United States has more than 450 national parks, with several in every state.

Many of them, like Mammoth Cave in this story, were created to protect remarkable parts of nature, such as caves, mountains, canyons, seashores, forests, and prairies. Other parks were created to protect places that have been important to the people of America, such as the Statue of Liberty welcoming immigrants in New York City's harbor. Still others protect places where important events in America's history happened or important people lived.

Each park was created because someone realized it was a precious place—a place every American should be able to visit, learn from, and appreciate. For example, miners once dug up the land where the spectacular Mammoth Cave system is located to find minerals for gunpowder. Now the lands are kept in their natural state so that people can enjoy them long into the future.

Making a park sometimes meant that people in the area had to move. Eminent domain is a law that allows the government to claim land from private owners if the land is needed for an important public use. Land has been claimed not only for parks but also for highways, railroads, power plants, reservoirs, and pipelines. The government can't just take the land; it must pay a fair price to the owner. Still, as Kit sees in the story, owners may not be happy about having to sell, and tenants, like the Bransons in the story, get no payment but still must move.

Many of the features in our national parks were built during Kit's time. Workers in the Civilian Conservation Corps, or CCC, were hired by the government to pave roads, construct bridges and trails, and build shelters. The CCC program, started by President Franklin Roosevelt during the Great Depression, provided work for thousands of people in desperate need of jobs, and made it possible for more people to visit and enjoy public lands.

It's still possible to see—and use—many of the attractive park features built by workers like Kit's brother, Charlie. If you visit a national park, ask a ranger to tell you about places in the park that were built by CCC crews. Then climb a winding stairway path, cross a sturdy footbridge, or relax on a stone bench overlooking a beautiful view. You won't have to imagine what Kit would have seen or felt long ago. Thanks to the national park system, which has protected these areas for generations of children and adults to enjoy, things will still be pretty much the same.

Read more of KIT'S stories,

available from booksellers and at *americangirl.com*

✿ *Classics* ✿

Kit's classic series, now in two volumes:

Volume 1:
Read All About It!

Kit has a nose for news. When the Great Depression hits home, Kit's newsletters begin making a real impact.

Volume 2:
Turning Things Around

With Dad still out of work, Kit wonders if things will ever get better. Could a letter to the newspaper make a difference?

✿ *Journey in Time* ✿

Travel back in time—and spend a day with Kit.

Full Speed Ahead

Help Kit outwit Uncle Hendrick, find a missing puppy, and stay out of jail when she's caught riding a freight train like a hobo! You get to choose your own path through this multiple-ending story.

✿ *Mysteries* ✿

Suspense and sleuthing with Kit.

The Jazzman's Trumpet: A Kit Mystery

A valuable trumpet goes missing. Can Kit prove *she's* not the thief?

Intruders at Rivermead Manor: A Kit Mystery

When Kit takes a part-time job helping an old woman in a rundown mansion, she finds clues to the past . . . and the future!

Parents, request a FREE catalogue at
americangirl.com/catalogue.
Sign up at **americangirl.com/email** to receive the latest
news and exclusive offers.

A Sneak Peek at

Intruders at Rivermead Manor

A Kit Mystery

Step into another suspenseful
adventure with Kit.

KIT KITTREDGE HURRIED along the sidewalk, feet crunching crisp autumn leaves. It was early October, and the trees were a blaze of color. Smoke curled from the chimneys of some of the grand houses in Uncle Hendrick's neighborhood. Her own house, Kit knew, would have a cheerful fire as her mother prepared the evening meal for the boarders who lived there, but Uncle Hendrick's house was never cheerful.

Kit sighed, hitching her schoolbag onto her shoulder. Last month, when Uncle Hendrick had complained that his arthritis was worse and he needed someone to look after him, he had asked for Kit. Mrs. Kittredge pointed out that there were plenty of women desperate for work these days. She suggested he hire one to help out until he felt better. But Uncle Hendrick had hired Kit to help out before, and he said she got the job done. Kit was happy to have the job, even though her great-uncle was often grumpy and his elegant house always felt cold.

So now, Kit walked to Uncle Hendrick's house after school several days a week and came home two hours later with the coins he paid her for her work. She was pleased to hand the money over to Mother. Times were hard, and money was scarce. Kit's family had nearly become homeless when her father lost his job. Their decision to turn their home into a boarding house had kept them going. For the past two years there had been lodgers to feed, rooms to clean, and extra laundry to do, but the whole family pulled together. Kit's father worked part-time at the airport now. The rest of the time he helped with the boarding house. Kit's older brother, Charlie, sent money home from Montana, where he worked for the National Park Service.

Wealthy Uncle Hendrick, who had never approved of Kit's family's taking in boarders, didn't understand about being poor. The gracious old homes in his neighborhood were large and elegant. There were hardly any signs of the Depression on

Uncle Hendrick's street at all, Kit thought. Except for the house next door to his.

Kit stopped at that house as she always did and peered through the wrought-iron gate. When the afternoon sun hit the colorful panes of glass in the center window, the glass glinted like a large eye, winking. But aside from the pretty window, the house did not look inviting at all. The tall boxwood hedge around the property was overgrown. The lawn was full of weeds. The vegetable patch was tangled. The brick house seemed like a once-grand lady whose gown had faded. This house looked as if it understood about the Great Depression, Kit thought.

She started walking again, then stopped short. *What was that sound?* There—it came again. A mewing cry. Could a kitten be lost in the tangles of the overgrown garden?

Over a year ago, Kit had taken in a stray dog— a large basset hound that she named Grace. Grace had been homeless and sad, but she soon became a loved and pampered pet. If Kit found a homeless kitten now, would Mother let her keep it?

Kit moved back to the gate. "Here, kitty, kitty!" she called. The quavering cry came again, louder now, and this time it sounded less like a cat and more like a human.

"Hello?" called Kit.

A weak voice answered, "Help! Over here!"

Kit fumbled to lift the latch. She pushed hard to swing the gate open. The voice called again, sounding even weaker. She followed the voice across the grass to the hedge, and then gasped at what she saw.

An elderly woman lay sprawled on the grass, one leg twisted beneath her. "Oh dear!" exclaimed Kit, kneeling to help the woman sit up. The woman's white hair straggled out of its bun, and her watery blue eyes blinked at Kit.

She reached out a hand and groped in the grass. Kit found her spectacles lying just inches away. The woman smiled gratefully and set the spectacles on her nose.

"Thank you," the woman said. "It's my ankle. I've turned it. If you hadn't heard me calling, I'd probably have lain here all night until the postman came tomorrow." Then she murmured something under her breath, something Kit could barely hear: "Or until one of the travelers found me . . ."

"Travelers?" asked Kit. "Do you mean hobos?" Homeless people sometimes went through nice neighborhoods asking for work. One of them might have assisted this old woman if Kit had not heard her.

The woman shook her head and smiled faintly. "No, not hobos. But never mind. You've found me, and I'm safe now. So tell me who you are, and how you happened to be passing by just when I needed rescuing!"

"I'm Kit Kittredge. And I'm on my way to my uncle's house next door. He's my great-uncle, actually. My mother's uncle."

The woman peered at Kit. "Oh! Then you're the one I've seen sweeping his front steps and hanging out his laundry. A hardworking girl." Her blue eyes narrowed. "I'll wager the old codger's paying you less than half of what you're worth. He's a skinflint! Always has been!" Then she smiled at Kit again and held out one thin hand. "Very pleased to meet you, dear girl. I'm Miss Elsie Mundis of Rivermead Manor."

About the Author

MARY CASANOVA is the author of numerous books for American Girl. To write this mystery, she spent time exploring Mammoth Cave National Park—aboveground and deep below. When she's not writing—or traveling to do research or to speak at schools and conferences—she's likely to be reading a good book, horse-back riding, or hiking with her husband, three dogs, and—on occasion—their two adventurous cats in the north woods of Minnesota.